£1.99
mc 31

CW00872196

PEBBLE IN A POOL

WILLIAM TAYLOR

alyson books
los angeles | new york

ALL CHARACTERS IN THIS BOOK ARE FICTITIOUS. ANY RESEMBLANCE TO REAL INDIVIDUALS—EITHER LIVING OR DEAD—IS STRICTLY COINCIDENTAL.

© 2003 BY WILLIAM TAYLOR. ALL RIGHTS RESERVED.

MANUFACTURED IN THE UNITED STATES OF AMERICA.

THIS TRADE PAPERBACK ORIGINAL IS PUBLISHED BY ALYSON PUBLICATIONS,
P.O. BOX 4371, LOS ANGELES, CALIFORNIA 90078-4371.
DISTRIBUTION IN THE UNITED KINGDOM BY TURNAROUND PUBLISHER SERVICES LTD.,
UNIT 3, OLYMPIA TRADING ESTATE, COBURG ROAD, WOOD GREEN,
LONDON N22 6TZ ENGLAND.

FIRST EDITION: JANUARY 2003

03 04 05 06 07 **a** 10 9 8 7 6 5 4 3 2 1

ISBN 1-55583-735-2

LIBRARY OF CONGRESS CATALOGING-IN-PUBLICATION DATA
TAYLOR, WILLIAM, 1938–
  PEBBLE IN A POOL / WILLIAM TAYLOR.—1ST ED.
  ISBN 1-55583-735-2
    1. HIGH SCHOOL STUDENTS—FICTION. 2. GAY TEENAGERS—FICTION. 3. TEENAGE
BOYS—FICTION. I. TITLE
PR9639.3.T35 P4 2002
823'.914—DC21   2002032989

COVER PHOTOGRAPHY BY STUDIO 1435.

for Carmen Gravatt,
with love

CHAPTER ONE

Toss a pebble into a pool of still water. Watch the ripples. Calculate the effect. Nothing much, I hear you say, just a few tiny waves and then all is still again. Well, think a bit harder. What if you were an amoeba living your single-cell life in that puddle, busy in the middle of your process of dividing? What if you were some higher form of life, a water bug, whatever, and those ripples caught you in a frenzy of water bug mating? Not quite so inconsequential now, I think. The effect of that pebble, tossed into the middle of that small, still pool—your home— might indeed be cataclysmic, catastrophic. At the very least, life-changing.

The problem in relating all this to my life of late is that I am not too sure at all whether I am the pebble, the pool, or some denizen of that water. But I can't think of any better way to open the story of my life as it has been lived over the course of last year. I had thought of those well-known lines from Shakespeare's *Julius Caesar:* "There is a tide in the affairs of men, / Which, taken at the flood, leads on to fortune; / Omitted, all the voyage of their life, / Is bound in shallows and in miseries." They're quite good lines, another watery analogy...well, maybe they are OK, but I'm rather uncertain about the shallows and miseries bit.

July was a bad month for my school. Everton High is certainly not the best high school in the world, and Everton is far, far from being the best small town. My last year at that school, and quite likely my last year in the town. I could have seen it out, served the rest of my time that year as comfortably as I had the 17-and-a-half years before. For reasons that even today I don't fully understand, I chose not to. I chose to stand up, open my mouth, and then...well, that's this story.

July was a bad month for three pupils in the senior class at Everton High: two dead and one almost dead.

At the beginning of that fateful month Lauren Brook died when Adrian Vanderlaar's car failed to take a corner and took out an oak tree instead. It was late one night...well, very early one morning, after what everyone said was a wild party that Lauren had not wanted to leave until virtually forced by Adrian. Adrian Vanderlaar—sportsperson, party person, drinker, smoker, and class stud—is now a vegetable in Everton Hospital. I saw the car. It seems poor Lauren copped the oak tree and Adrian got shot through the windscreen to be sandwiched somehow between his car and part of the tree that fell.

When the most popular blond couple in a school gets whacked, all hell breaks loose. Everton High is no exception. The school was assembled and stood for a minute's silence in memory of Lauren while her image was projected on a giant screen at the front of the hall. People stood up and talked about what a wonderful person she had been, an inspiration to us all. Others stood up to say she would never be forgotten. We prayed for the unlikely recovery of Adrian and also for both families. No mention was made of the alcohol levels—astronomic—in the blood of Lauren or that of Adrian. Naturally, no mention was made of the fact that Adrian had always referred to his car as his babe-bonking bus.

Those who felt in need got grief counseling from a team of weird women who set up a grief counseling shop in a little room behind the cafeteria. Their business ran for a good 10 days, until even Mr. Sparks, our principal, realized it was less a counseling operation and more a great chance to get out of class and relax and chat over a free slice of cake, a free cup of coffee, and a free box of tissues. Needless to say, the school closed for the afternoon of Lauren's funeral.

For a few days at least, there were queues of those, mainly girls, waiting to sit beside the bed of poor battered Adrian as he lay in an induced coma. Because any signs of his coming-back to even half-life were minimal and his doctors kept on inducing the coma—and also because, black, blue, bloodied, battered, and with a shaven head, he was unrecognizable—the queues soon shortened and then petered out altogether. Adrian's future as a stud (or as anything else, for that matter) seemed to be well and truly over. Adrian became a villain, which, of course, he was!

Life at Everton High returned to as near normal as ever it was. Two, three weeks at most and Lauren was talked about in the past tense; Adrian, not at all.

Then came the end of July and my life changed, and I have no one else to blame—or to thank for it—than myself.

Spike Messenger, also of my class, got his head bashed in with a blunt instrument by person or persons unknown and was left, dead, in a pool of his own blood and excrement, in a gutter of one of Everton's less well-lit backstreets.

A special assembly of the school was not called. Instead, Spike got a brief mention two days later at our regular, scheduled, ordinary, weekly school assembly. There was no blown-up pic of poor old Spike. There was no talk at all of grief counseling or cake and coffee. A very brief mention—until I stood up and made it much longer.

I will never ever know precisely what made me do it. I didn't like Spike. There were times when Spike had made my flesh creep. He was everything I knew a guy should never be. Loud, in-your-face, flamboyant, a weirdo of the very first order and an insult to any decent normal guy. Only God knows how Spike Messenger had managed to survive as long as he had in our school, in our town. Spike Messenger was gay.

Like, well, we all knew Spike had bought it. It had been splashed across the front page of the *Everton Daily News*. BACK STREET FATALITY, it was headlined. There was a fuzzy pic of the crime scene with a heap of what had once been Spike covered with a blanket. Not that the paper had named him. "Police are withholding the name of the deceased until next-of-kin have been contacted" and then went on to say, "Foul play cannot be ruled out." Yeah, right!

Everton is not a big town. By the time the paper came out you would have had to be blind, deaf, or mute not to have known that Spike Messenger had been murdered and that the cops were busy searching for the blunt instrument used to hammer in his skull. Foul play could most certainly not be ruled out!

Principal Sparks lumbered to his feet, his usual gloomy look on his face. "It is my sad duty to draw to your attention the death of a pupil of this school, John Messenger." A bit more mumbling, and then, "I would fail in my responsibilities to you all if I did not point out the very real dangers of lurking around in dark backstreets late at night. Should you be fool enough to make this choice, you are looking for trouble. The choice of certain lifestyles is calculated to add to the risks you take. From this sad event let us all learn a lesson." Then Sparks lumbered back to his seat, sat down, and immediately started to whisper in the ear of his deputy, who normally got to speak next. It was these few moments of nothing happening that were to change my life.

It would be easy to say that I was incensed at the unfairness of it all. It would be easy to say that I was enraged at the glaring imbalance of Lauren versus Spike, or even of damaged Adrian versus Spike. It would be easy to say...well, any one of a dozen things, but in all truth, there wasn't time for conscious thinking. I suppose it was all of the foregoing—felt instinctively rather than worked through in my mind—which made me get to my feet and speak. I know hot and cold shivers were running through me, and I am sure I was shaking. I had never, ever done anything like this in my whole life.

"Er...er, Mr. Sparks, I just want to say something about Spike." I knew I was speaking too loudly and my voice was higher than it should have been. There wasn't a sound, but I sensed a sort of expectancy in the 600 kids surrounding me—and quite likely in the 30 or so teachers on the stage up front. "Spike Messenger was different from most of us. I am going to miss him about this place." Thinking back, I know that was a lie. Spike had been a right thorn in my side for some long time. "Spike showed us all that you could be different, and I think it is a great tragedy that it is quite likely because he was, well, a bit odd, that he got killed. No one deserves that, not Spike and not anyone else. Spike was a very bright guy indeed, and this means a great loss to us all, a loss to society, really. I know he could be a bit annoying at times." (Looking back, another lie.) "But he could certainly make us think about things."

I should have left it at that, but I didn't. New to public speaking, I said too much and broke just about every precept that had been drilled into me. "We all knew Spike Messenger was gay. Spike made no secret of that and he talked to me about it often. Well, it seems to me that it's not all that bad to be gay if, like Spike, you never hurt anyone else and just sort of, well, ask to live your life the way you want to. Spike has not been allowed to go on living his gay life, quite likely just because of what he was. That is wrong." I looked straight up at Principal Sparks. "I am going to ask everyone in this assembly here today to stand with me for a minute's silence in memory of Spike Messenger."

I certainly got the silence, but it took awhile to get them standing. I stood alone and looked up at old Sparks. He stared back at me. Then, slowly, he got to his feet. One by one his henchmen and henchwomen stood up and, gradually, there was a ripple around the hall; one or two of the kids, then more, began to stand. Then, like the flock of sheep they truly resembled, all of the others stood. In the long run, Spike Messenger actually got almost five minutes of silence, the only sounds being those of the flock shuffling to its feet.

"Thank you, Paul, for what you've said." And with this, Principal Sparks dismissed the assembly.

In truth, I don't think I had said all that much. I had not mentioned Spike Messenger's multicolored and spiked hair that had given him his nickname. I had not mentioned Spike Messenger threatening to take the school to the Human Rights Commission unless they let him try out to be a cheerleader. Maybe I should have mentioned that glorious day when poor old Spike turned up at school wearing a copy of that famous red dress worn by the late, great Marilyn Monroe. I really should have mentioned the number of times Spike Messenger had had his head shoved down toilets, clean and unclean, and how, once or twice, I had even been one of those who had enjoyed the show.

In spite of what was omitted, I do know that Paul Carter, son of the well-known pastor of the New Life Church, should have said nothing at all...should have kept his mouth shut and his thoughts to himself!

Certainly not for the first time in my life, I got to hear—hissed, muttered, or otherwise flung—those very well-known words: "fag," "faggot," "homo," "queen," "queer," "pansy," and others even worse. But certainly it was the first time in my life I had heard them flung at me as a weapon designed to wound. I know it was not my imagination that an actual physical dimension now distanced me from all the others as we left that assembly. It was tangible. I could feel the menace. A good 10 or 15 feet separated me, the new pariah, from those moving along nearest to me. It was a strange feeling; after all, I had always been at least a peripheral member of the gang.

I left the place.

CHAPTER TWO

All this was nothing compared with what came next. I got in my car and drove out of the town and up into the hills, parked in a deserted and freezing-cold spot, sat, shivered, and chewed my fingernails. I knew I had done nothing wrong. I knew in my heart that I had done the right thing. Equally, I knew I had broken some sort of code, and I most certainly knew that a price was to be paid for that breaking. At that moment I did not quite know just how high a price that was to be and just how soon I had to start paying. Common sense should have told me all this, but common sense had deserted me when I stood up in that assembly. I had no one else to blame other than myself.

Darkness and a thick, misty drizzle fell as I drove home.

They were waiting. All four of them. Mum, Daniel, my younger brother, and Hannah, my younger sister—the three of them lined up behind my father. That my father was beside himself with rage and on the point of exploding was obvious. The storm broke before I even had a chance to drop my backpack.

"An abomination in the eyes of the Living God..." And he flung himself upon me and flat-handed me across one cheek. I gasped at the shock of the stinging pain and went to put up an arm to defend myself. He didn't give me a chance, as he dealt similarly to my other cheek, screaming, "Giving yourself over to fornication and going after strange flesh," his fist smashing into my cheek. The pain stung and stunned; so did my father's ferocity.

"No no no Den Denny Dennis..." my mother tried.

"Shut your mouth, woman," he yelled, and he bashed me again. "This...this...this..." but words didn't quite fail him. "This slime, this worm from the pits of hell, this spawn of Satan..." He was beside himself with rage.

I made yet another mistake. I was trembling—from fear as much as from the pain and sting of his blows. I shook and I giggled insanely and found some part of my voice. "Satan, Father? I thought I was spawn of yours and..."

At which he kicked me viciously, brutally hard; he kicked at my knees and I staggered, tried to regain balance, failed, fell to the ground, and then he was on me in a frenzied attack, kicking, kneeing, punching, and pulling at me, hammering right into me with all of his considerable strength and in a fury that knew no bounds.

I lay there and took it. All of it. I made no effort whatsoever to defend myself against my father other than to curl into a self-protective and probably fetal ball, my hands and arms doing their best to protect my head, face, genitals. Small protection.

God knows how long it lasted. It seemed like an eternity. Probably no more than three, four minutes, until the main force of his physical fury abated and he pulled himself away, gasping for breath, eyes bulging, the veins of his face and neck engorged, deeply reddened.

I managed to pull myself from him and to feel for, find, and pull myself up to rest, sitting against a wall.

For all this time my mother, brother, and sister were nothing more than a frozen tableau of bit players in the background. I gasped for breath, and I caught my mother's eye and looked into her face. White as a sheet, almost ghostlike, trembling, she looked away from me. My sister stood, eyes downcast, staring at the ground. The glint and gleam in my brother Daniel's eye, and the very faintest trace of a well-controlled grin on his face, told me something else again!

If I thought my father was finished, I was mistaken. The physical battle may have been over, but the outpouring of righteous fury had only just begun. "You...you have brought shame and dishonor on my name, on the name of your mother and on this house. 'There shall be no whore of the daughters of Israel, nor a sodomite of the sons of Israel,' " the pastor intoned.

This was, at least, less painful! I had heard it all, Sunday after Sunday, for the whole of my life.

"That you...you foul creature have done this to me! You filth. You utter filth." It seemed he was gathering his strength, so I edged myself a little further up the wall and into a corner. My head throbbed with pain where my brow was cut, and blood dripped over my hands and onto the carpet. I have no idea if I was crying. I guess I was. And still he didn't stop, " 'And in hell he lift his eyes, and he cried and said, 'Have mercy upon me...' Ha! There is no mercy for flesh like yours! Filth!"

"But—" I found my voice.

"Shut your foul and filthy mouth!" He gave me no chance. "Keep your filth, your foulness for others like yourself. Keep your vile contamination from us." His arm swept around to encompass the rest of my family. "After all we have done for you! You...!" Words failed him for a moment.

Dazed, bewildered, battered, and bruised, I didn't even try anymore.

"Shall I serve the meal now, Dennis?" I heard my mother's timidly whispered question.

"Be still, woman." My father had no intention of letting up just yet. "Be still, do you hear me?"

"What..." I tried to speak. "What have—" But he gave me no chance.

"Keep your vile words to yourself. Save them for those who, like yourself, offend God's ordinance and His very name. Save them for the likes of that evil scum in whose praise you spoke and whose blood was shed as payment for his deviance." He glared down at me. "You...you are no longer a son of mine, no longer a son of this house..."

"Den...Dennis..." from my mother.

"You will get out of this house now and forever! You are not my son. This is not your home. Pack your filthy rubbish and get out. Out! You'll stay here not a moment longer, spreading your filth and disease to your brother, your sister. Out! *Out!* Do you hear me, you swine?"

"No. No, Dennis," came a moan from my mother.

"I'll tell you again, woman! Shut your mouth! This is not your business," and he turned to her, raising a hand.

At which I found my voice and some little strength. I struggled to stand, saying as I forced myself to my feet. "Don't...don't you touch her...I'll...I'll..."

"You'll what?" A sneer.

"Leave her...leave them alone. I'll go. I'll get out."

"This instant. Now!" And he pointed to the door, clearly forgetting my filthy rubbish.

My mother hadn't. She found courage from somewhere, and I was given half an hour to quit the only home I had ever known.

The last thing I heard as I picked up my pack and left the room was the voice of my brother, Daniel. "Can I have his room now that he's gone, Dad?"

I saw none of them again that night. Backpack, sports bag, three plastic bags I found in the bathroom, and because I could find nothing else I could vaguely call my own, the two pillow slips from my bed. Clothes, footwear, sleeping bag, books, my little cheap stereo and the half dozen CDs I had accumulated, a few odds and ends of treasures, and my toothbrush. A pathetic and jumbled heap. I stowed the lot, made two trips out to my old car, took one final look around my room, stole a blanket that wasn't mine, and then left. I drove back up into the hills to the same place I had been after the school assembly, parked the car, and tried to think.

Pain flooded my body, but it was just about bearable. The pain in my head was something else. I think I was in a state of shock. I felt dazed, sick, shuddering, shaking uncontrollably, almost helpless. I guess too that I was hungry, and I certainly needed something to drink. I didn't really know what to do or where to go. There was no one at all I could think of to whom I might turn for help. Life for the eldest kid—well, former eldest kid—of the pastor of the New Life Church had been very restricted indeed. I had no close school friends. Well, truth to tell, I probably now had not even a friendly acquaintance. Summed up: For me, life had revolved around home, church, school, and the part-time job that at least meant I had my car to live in at this moment of great need.

My part-time job saved me. I don't know what time it was, but it got far too cold to stay in my car, and besides, I desperately needed something to drink and something to eat. Neither the glove box nor the floor of the car yielded anything near edible, and I decided to drive back down and into the town.

For two years now I had pumped gas, working Friday nights and all day Saturday for Arvin Singh, owner of the Eastside Service Station. He was a good boss. I was reliable. I was lucky to have the job; had never realized, of course, just how lucky.

I had the keys to the place because I opened it up at 6 on Saturday mornings while Arvin was still tucked up in bed with Mrs. Singh. Generally, I would run the whole operation, single-handedly, for three or four hours before Arvin remembered he had responsibilities.

Weeknights the place closed around 7. I'd let myself in, make myself coffee, help myself to something edible and, perhaps, just curl up in a corner of the little staff room and maybe try to think of where to go and what to do next. Might sound simple, but in all truth, I only half knew what I was doing.

The place, as I knew it would be, was hidden in darkness. I parked behind the building, looked around to see if anyone might be lurking. It wasn't the better part of town, and I thought a brief thought of poor Spike Messenger. The coast was clear and I let myself in. Some of the fog in my head started to lift as I drank my coffee, but almost at the same time as the fog was lifting, I started to shiver uncontrollably. A full-body shaking. I crawled into my sleeping bag, but it made very little difference. I could not stop shaking and, quite simply, I couldn't think. For the first time I started to cry. What had happened? What had I done? Where was I? Where could I go? What, for God's sake, could I do? Round and round and round in my mind, my head.

I didn't hear the key in the lock nor the door open. The light switched on. "Wha..." A sort of squawk and I sprang back, almost defensively, half out of my sleeping bag now, into a corner.

"What the...Jesus Christ!" and Steven Peterson, tenant of the old workshop that was part of Arvin Singh's premises, knelt down beside me. "God Almighty, what's happened to you?"

I just shivered and shook and looked into his face. I couldn't say anything. I just couldn't get one word out.

"Hang on," and Steve got to his feet, moved to the door, opened it, and looked up and down the backyard; closed, locked the door and came back to me. "They didn't...not whoever it was did for that poor kid? No. Shit, no."

I shook my head and managed to say "No."

"Let me look," and he didn't wait for a reply. Quickly, efficiently, he peeled back my sleeping bag, examined my body, my head, all over. I couldn't have done a thing to stop him even had I wanted. I just lay back in that corner and let him check me all over. Steve Peterson looked very grim. "What, then? Who? Come on, Paul, snap out of it. Who did this to you?"

I swallowed, looked at him again, and said, "My father."

"Jesus Christ," he repeated, sat back on his haunches, scratched his head for a moment. "Better get you to the hospital. Better see a doctor...whew, and I reckon I better call the cops."

These words sure served to bring me back to life. I dragged myself up the wall and stood, looking down on him. "No," very definitely. "No. Don't need to go the hospital. I'll be all right...I'll be all right. And you're not calling the cops. No, not that. Look," and I moved around a bit, wincing only very slightly, "I'm fine."

"Your father did this to you?" Steve spoke very slowly.

I nodded. "Yes."

"The bastard. The bastard!"

"No no no no..." I shook my head. "No. You got it all wrong. My father did what he thought was right. My father had a right, he did. The father has a right to chastise a child."

"Oh, dear God...don't hand me that crap. Why, for heaven's sake? Why...oh," and he let out a sigh. "Should've known." He gave a sort of cross between a bark and a laugh. "That bastard. Man of God, your old man? Bloody Nazi, more like." Steve looked at me. "He heard what you did at school today? Right?"

"Yes. How did you know what I did?"

He smiled at me. "It's a small town, Bozo. Everyone knows. Good news travels fast, eh?"

"Good news?"

"Good news, bad news, any sort of news in this place. Sit

down, for chrissake. Tell me what happened." He held up a hand as I opened my mouth. "And don't argue. Tell me. Tell me the lot while I make us both a coffee—although, God knows, you could do with something stronger. No, maybe not. Could be concussed. Didn't check that. I'll do it now." And he did. "Don't think so, but how the hell would I know? I'm not a bloody medic. Anyway, you talk. I'll do the coffee and clean you up a bit."

So I told him the lot. It seemed to help. I stopped shaking, but my head still ached. It ached even more after Steve had a go at cleaning the two or three places where blood had dried over a few of the damaged bits. The coffee warmed me, and then, all of a sudden, I felt so tired.

"OK, man. Better be getting you home then."

That brought me up with a round turn. "No. No, no, no. I told you that. Can't go home...won't go, not ever, won't go back there."

"Shut up and simmer down, you bloody little fool," said Steve, pleasantly. He smiled at me, took out his cigarettes, lit one, and blew a cloud of smoke all over me. "You're coming home with me. Chuck me your car keys. I'll get the rest of your shit out of your car and lock it up. Really should take you to the quack, but I'm not going to drag you there. A hot shower and a good night of sleep and, come tomorrow, we'll have a think about what happens next." He looked at me and gave a slight, tight smile. "Hey?"

"What?" I was beyond argument.

"You did a good thing today, man. The right thing."

"Did I?" As I looked at him, I broke down completely and howled my eyes out. Steve Peterson came to me, said nothing, took me in his arms, and held me tight.

CHAPTER THREE

I have little memory of what happened next. I was not really conscious of my surroundings, of where I was taken or very much about what was done for me. Exhaustion took its toll, and rather than doing anything for myself, I allowed another to take charge and do everything for me. I'm pretty sure I was given something to eat and another hot drink. I also know I was shoved under a shower, because the sting of the hot water on my raw bits and pieces was nearly as bad as the inflicting of the wounds in the first place! I do know I was wrapped up in a long, white towelling robe, because that is what I was wearing when I woke up, very late, the next morning.

"OK, fella? Thought I heard you stirring. Here's a coffee for you. Now, then, if I'm not satisfied that the damage to your bashed-up frame is only superficial, I fully intend to hog-tie you and cart you off to the doc. Understand?"

I nodded. "Yeah, OK. And...um...thanks for the coffee and um...er...thanks for—"

"Oh, shut up! Now get out of bed, strip off, and show me what you've got!" Steve ordered.

I know I blushed. But I did as I was told. "Look. See. I'm fine." Only a slight lie. I knew there was no damage that wouldn't repair quickly. Mind you, when I caught sight of myself in a mirror, the shock was something else! "Wow!"

"Yeah. Bloody awful, eh?" Steve smiled. "All right." He looked me up and down. "I'm not entirely satisfied. You got some pretty nasty bruises and cuts, man. That one on your knee and the upper thigh." He nodded. "And your..." He looked me in the eye. "What would you call 'em...your er...private parts have taken a bit of a booting, but at least they're all there. How do you feel around the ribs? You'd certainly know if one was fractured."

"Just a little bit sore."

"I'm not surprised. I've seen one or two hammerings in my time but...oh, well. Shit happens, as the bishop said to the nun. Walk up and down a bit...right. Now come here."

This guy could sure give orders! "What now?"

"Waggle your fingers for me."

"Why?"

Steve shook his head and tried to swallow a smile. "Do as you're bloody told. Now your toes. Oh, all right. You're largely in one piece, but I've got a few doubts about the inside of your head."

"So have I," I said, and grinned.

"Ah. That's what I needed to see," and he slapped me on the shoulder. "Oops! Sorry." He laughed.

"No, you're not."

"Yeah, right. I'm not. OK, man. I've got to get into town for a couple of hours. Just make the place your own, find something to eat. I'm not going to wait on you hand and foot. Just find your way around everything."

"I should be packing up and heading—"

"Do you ever listen? No. Don't bother answering. At your age no one does. You are not packing up and heading off anywhere in the near future. You are OK here. You are OK with me. Yes, you are a mountain of trouble and a right bloody pain in the butt." He smiled broadly. "You know what I am saying."

"Thank you" was all I could say.

"You've done me a good turn or two, Paul. It won't hurt me to repay just a little bit of the help you've given me. Now I'm off. Oh, the cat and the dog. Just have a chat to them. The cat's name is Mr. Cat and the dog's name is Audrey. They won't bite. Well, I lie, the bloody cat probably will! See you sometime early this afternoon...and then we can have a talk about what comes next. Right?"

"Thank you," I said again.

"Stop thanking me." And Steven Peterson took off.

I took Steve at his word and made myself at home. It would be nice to say that, in this sort of calm after the storm, that the clouds had cleared in more ways than one. But they hadn't. I felt a sickness, fear, apprehension in my gut that would not go away. I certainly felt physically sore all over, but that was, in all truth, the least of my worries. And neither had the weather improved. There was still a thick, grey misty cold drizzle that matched my mood and the way I felt.

I explored Steven Peterson's home. About seven or eight miles from the town, it stood on a rise, trees all around it and right at the end of a winding, hilly, and unsealed road. Old Quarry Road. The old quarry, long disused, was these days home to hundreds, if not thousands, of rabbits. The house itself didn't take much exploring. It was small, square, and very plain. It was also very tidy. Old, it was clearly a house that Steve, or someone else, had modernized and done up, rebuilt, renovated. It only had four main rooms: a living and sitting room, a kitchen–cum–dining room, and two quite big bedrooms—the one I had used and the other that was obviously Steve's. There was a sort of a tacked-on bathroom. Around the whole house ran a verandah that was used, obviously, for a stack of firewood and for lounging on. It also seemed to be home for his pets, Mr.

Cat and Audrey: a sleek, pantherlike jet-black cat and a very old dog of indescribable breed. I said hello to the two of them just so that they knew I was around. They ignored me. This suited me just fine, because I had never been much into pet animals, particularly cats.

The house was warm. A wood-burning stove was freestanding between the living and kitchen areas, and served to warm up the whole place nicely, cozily. I fed it some more wood. The four rooms were all painted a pale-cream color. The floors were wooden. They looked old. The boards had been sanded and polished, and there were very bright floor rugs scattered around all of the rooms, with one or two even tacked up on the walls. There was a decent stereo; a pile of CDs, mostly classical stuff; a small television; a large bookcase; a few ornaments and ashtrays; and a couple of vividly painted pictures that meant nothing to me. No photos or junk like that. There was one surprising feature for a guy like Steve, your sort of real he-man. In the middle of a wooden coffee table was a blue bowl jammed full of spring flowers. It looked very nice indeed.

I made myself a couple of slices of toast and choked them down. Wasn't hard to find where the obvious things were kept! Switched from coffee to tea, and sat down and thought about the guy who was going out of his way to help me.

I had helped him? Almost news to me. A very little help indeed. Poor old Steve. All I had done was save him from his computer, and he had well and truly repaid that favor before any of this stuff happened to me.

Steve Peterson leased a couple of workshops from Arvin Singh. He had just taken over the place when I started work for Arvin two, going on three years back. I didn't know Steve, not really. Had never ever talked to him on a personal level. He had always kept a distance between himself and others—and I was no exception. Not that I had been all that interested. I had no idea where he came from. No idea even how old he might be. Could have been an old-looking 25 or a young-looking 40. He was certainly a very good-looking older dude. A head of shaggy brown hair, well-built—reckon just under six foot, about the same height as me—athletic and with a nice face that was made even better because of his eyes. Never seen a guy or a girl, anyone at all, with eyes like Steve's. Dark—a deep, dark blue—big, and even more set off by a forest of thick eyelashes. I don't often go around looking at people's eyes, but Steven Peterson's eyes were amazing. It was his eyes that made people look at him. He had a few bad habits, but I reckon most people do. He used language that would make a trooper blush, nonstop, and he smoked, also just about nonstop.

Steve made quite a spectacular living by turning old and broken furniture into works of art. He took old battered stuff, worked on it, and sold it for a fortune.

I knew he made a fortune, because I had done his books for a year, 18 months maybe, because he was frightened of his computer. Yes. This dude who seemed to have it all was terrified of something as simple as a computer.

I had come to know him enough to pass the time of day. Whenever Arvin made me take a break, I'd go out the back of the gas station, sit in the sun, and enjoy a coffee, a Coke, whatever. Sometimes when I was out there Steve would come out, plonk himself down beside me, and light a cigarette and take a break himself. We would pass the time of day, chat briefly, nothing more than that. It wasn't until one day when Arvin asked me to take some papers through to him about the property he was renting that I got to know him a little bit better.

Poor old Steve was near-hysterical in front of his computer. His hair stood on end, and he kept on combing his fingers through it so it spiked straight up. He wore glasses that made his eyes seem ever bigger. He looked like a startled, scared little boy. The boy had been smoking one cigarette after another, judging by the ashtray, and the room was filled with a shifting grey haze. The place stank of smoke. His normal level of pretty blunt language was quite unprintable.

"I'll kill the fuckin' thing," he yelled at me. "Reckon I have killed it. It's bloody stone dead." He dropped his head onto the keyboard. "All that bloody work," he muttered. "Touched one bloody key and the whole stuffing mess has gone. All that work down the sodding drain."

"What's wrong?" I enquired stupidly.

He told me in no uncertain terms, his level of desperation and his look of absolute despair saying it all. In short, Steven Peterson was a computer klutz. "Let me have a go," I said.

"Do what you like with the bloody thing. Screw its nuts off, stab it in its guts with a rusty knife, chuck it out the window. These things were never designed for a decent man to use! Here. Sit down. I need a smoke."

I thought the better of telling him that was the last thing he needed! I sat down. "What programme are you running?" and then added very quickly when I saw the look in his eye, "Nah. Doesn't matter. I think I know." I clicked through a few options, and within 30 seconds everything came back on-screen. "There we are," I said. "It's back."

"What the hell did you do? It's a bloody miracle!" Steve blinked through the smoke haze.

"Hmmm," I said, looking at the screen and then at him. I didn't like to tell him that what I had rescued looked for all the world like something a sick dog had puked up. I guess my look must have told him what I was thinking!

"Don't you look at me in that pitying way, you smart-arse

little bastard." He was grinning as he said it.

I really did have to laugh at him, but not too much. I looked at the screen. "You got a bit of a problem, eh? I think you better tell me what you are trying to do."

He did. We had a chat. Then he offered me the job of doing his books and said he thought it would take me about 20 hours a week and he would pay me quite well. I told him I couldn't afford 20 hours a week, even at a very high rate of pay. "Look," and I did smile at him. "I can do what you need doing in about one hour a week and I can do it for you after I have finished working for Arvin."

"Shoot!" he said. "What you going to charge me? I've heard all about you computer dicks. Charge like wounded bulls."

"It's next to nothing you need done. I like doing it. I am not going to charge you anything at all. You can buy me a Coke or something if you want to," I said.

Which is how I got to know that Steven Peterson made a very fine living from his old furniture. I didn't get to know him very much better, because usually he left me to it with a heap of scribbled notes in something he called a scrapbook, along with a pile of receipts. Often he wasn't there at all when I did his stuff, and if he did pop in and try to make me take some money from him, I would just refuse what he offered. Generally, when I left, I would discover that he had topped up the gas tank of my car. It was good work to do and good practice for my accounting course at school. Steve made very sure that he learnt nothing more about computers.

CHAPTER FOUR

I was asleep on the sofa when Steve got back. He moved very quietly, but I woke, startled and none too sure of where I was. "Go back to sleep, man. No need for you to wake up."

"What time is it?"

He told me. "Just after 4. Took a bit longer than I thought."

"Shoot," I got to my feet. "I um...er, better be on my way."

"Sit down, dummy. You're going nowhere."

I looked out of the window. "There's my car. How did it get here?" I was still sort of half asleep.

"Well, it didn't drive itself. Lalita Singh drove it out. I took her home. That's why I'm a bit late back."

I sighed. "Thank you." I didn't know what to say. "I don't know what...I don't, I don't—"

"Listen to me, man." He looked through to the kitchen area. "You haven't had anything proper to eat, have you? Come through to the kitchen with me and I'll rustle us up something." The tone in his voice gave me no option. I followed. Steve went on talking. "You're hurting, both physically and up top, confused, and more than likely, shit-scared about what comes next. Let's get a few things straight. I'd like to leave this chat for a couple of days until you're feeling more yourself again, but I can see that isn't going to work." He dragged a stool out from the table and pointed to it. I sat. "Look, I can't force you to stay here, neither would I want to. You're a big boy now..."

"But—"

"Shut up, for chrissake. Listen! You're in the shit, you got nowhere to go. You're not fit to go anywhere after the hiding you've had. I'll make it simple," and he went on talking as he sorted out pans and pots, and broke a heap of eggs into a bowl. "You can stay here with me for as long as you like. Make this your home until you sort out in your mind what you are going to do. As you can see, there's plenty of room. As you can see, it's quite comfortable...and it sure as hell won't hurt me to have another body around the place."

"I can't stay here," I said. "I can't stay here and bludge off you. I got next to no money and only get what Arvin pays me for my day and a bit...and I reckon he won't want me anymore, not after all this."

Steve banged an empty frying pan onto the stove top and actually yelled at me. "If there was an unbruised spot on your battered body, I'd love to hit it! What the fuck is it you Bible bangers jabber on about, that shit about casting your bread on the waters and it'll be returned?"

" 'Cast thy bread upon the water: for thou shalt find it after many days.' Song of Solomon."

"That's the bugger," said Steve, calming down. "It's payback time, dumb ass. You've done your bit for me and now it's my turn. You've saved me a small fortune and—stupidly, I reckon—never taken a cent for it for...how long? A couple of years, nearly? You can stay here for as long as you like. Call it home if you will. If you try to give me a cent, well, I'll force it back down your throat. Geddit?"

A great weight lifted off me. I was in the right place at the right time and with the right person, or so it seemed. Did it really matter that this person constantly took the Lord's name in vain, used profanity that would surely see him frizzle in hell for eternity, and never seemed to stop smoking?

"Yes," I said in a small voice. "I get it. Thank you."

"Now get off your fat arse, get into the other room, and you should find half a bottle of wine somewhere on the bookcase. Left it there last night. Should be enough for a couple of glasses."

A drinker, too! "I don't drink."

"I wasn't offering you one! I meant two for me—now toss me that pack of smokes. And, by the way..."

"What?"

"Arvin and Lalita send you kind wishes, and I'm to tell you, if you don't want to stay here, there's a bed for you at their place—again, for as long as you like. Mind you, you'd be dumber than you look if you accepted. Those kids of theirs! Whew!"

He was right on that one. "I know what you mean," I said, with some feeling.

"And you're not to work this coming weekend. They insist on that, and..." He fossicked in a pocket. "Here's your pay packet. You'll find they've even paid you for not working. You really are a dumb bugger, you know. Alone in the world? You? Mr. Nice Guy? Now work out how to set the bloody table and, mark my words, you'll be doing the dishes no matter how sore you feel."

"It would be a great pleasure." I grinned and then winked at him.

Spike Messenger's body was released by the cops to his family. They held his funeral. I went. I had never liked Spike, but I do think that in some way I had at least appreciated him. I didn't want to go. I had to go. It was a strange event at some funeral chapel in the town. The place was packed, but there were not many locals. Spike's death had got a lot of attention in the press, on radio, and television. It was an odd funeral—not that I had ever been to many other than a few for old New Lifers who had passed on to a better world in God's kingdom. This one was nowhere near as happy as the ones I had been to before. Next to no flowers, no music other than some lousy fake stuff being piped in from somewhere. A miserable and mean little funeral, really. I just bet that old Spike would have designed something better for himself and, most certainly, wouldn't have wanted to get buried or barbecued in the plain wooden box they gave him. Spike would have painted himself and his coffin in all hues of the rainbow—and then some.

At Spike's funeral people just sort of stood up and spoke. It was almost as if there had been two different Spikes. People in his family, but not his mother or father, talked about a Spike who had been, really, just a regular guy. I guess they may have seen him that way and that's their business, but in all truth, Spike's red Marilyn dress hadn't been the only weird outfit in his wardrobe. No, his clothes were sure not the clothes of a regular guy. No one mentioned the bikini swimsuit (with a bra top, of course) he often wore during the summer. He obviously loved that bikini, because he often wore it—once or twice even out in the street! Be nice if they were letting him wear it in his coffin, but I bet they weren't. No one mentioned Spike's great love of hats and very elderly moth-eaten fur coats that he found in op shops and garage sales.

I don't think many, if any, of those who had come from other places to mourn Spike had even met him. They spoke less about Spike than about a whole long list of things to do with difference, the rights of people who may be a bit different, and naturally enough, how Spike's death diminished us all. Someone who had clearly known Spike a little bit began to go into a long story of Spike at a gay parade up in the city, dressed in a costume of yellow-and-pink feathers and diamonds in his hair, up on top of a float, miming Abba songs. This was more the Spike I knew, and I found the story quite interesting. I could just see Spike all dolled up and enjoying the attention. However, someone from Spike's own family nudged the old guy who was conducting the funeral, and the teller of the story of Spike at the parade was forced to cut short his fascinating tale. If a funeral is meant to be a kind of celebration of the life of the dead one, this affair was not going to be a celebration of the sort of life Spike had at least started to live.

Principal Sparks—at least he was there—did not stand up and say anything about his former pupil. I noticed two or three kids from school, but they weren't the usual kids I had anything to do with. I went back to Steve's place after Spike's funeral without having said a word to anyone. It was only when I got home—home?—that I realized that I could have got up and said something about Spike Messenger. But, this time, I hadn't. I don't think it really mattered.

Meanwhile, the cops had made no progress in their enquiries, and it was said they were nowhere near making an arrest. It seemed like Spike's killer or killers would get away scot-free.

CHAPTER FIVE

Bruises heal. I got better. Even the sick feeling in my gut disappeared, and it began to seem as if I had never lived anywhere else other than at Steven Peterson's place. No contact at all was made with me by anyone in my family. Nothing. It was as if I had never existed. My father was as good as his word; I had been fully cast out. Strange as it may seem, it didn't worry me very much. If I spared a thought for any one of them, it was for my mother. I hoped and, yes, I prayed that she was all right. Hannah too. The other two, the men of my family? To hell with both of them! They could look after themselves.

They must have found out where I was living. I was still at school, and I still worked for Arvin. I saw Daniel and Hannah at school. They must have seen me. I knew Hannah had. I bumped into her in the library. She jumped a foot in the air, looked the other way, and took off like a startled rabbit.

"You're not worried about it, are you?" Steve asked when I told him about Hannah.

"No. Dunno. I don't know. She is my sister."

"To hell with the whole damn lot of 'em," said Steve.

"You got that one wrong. The whole lot are going to heaven."

"Don't start on that crap. After what your sod of an old man did to you, he's bound for deepest, darkest, and hottest hell with the er...swine or whatever."

"You got that one wrong too," I grinned. "He did what he

thought was right, my father. You don't understand. The man is the head of the house. It is his right."

Steve stopped what he was doing and looked at me. "Did he ever do anything like that to you before?"

"You mean, give me a beating?"

"You know what I mean."

"A few times. Yes. Generally, I asked for it."

"Oh, yeah? Stand up, did you, and say, 'Daddy, please beat the shit out of me'? Pull the other one. What about your brother and sister?"

"We all got it occasionally. Generally, with his belt."

"Your mother?" Very quietly.

I looked away and muttered, "Well, not with his belt."

"Holy shit!" said Steve. "Bastard!"

"Not in front of us. Just, well, sometimes I'd hear him yelling and her crying and then hear...doesn't matter. Drop it."

"How did he get into that crackpot religion shit?"

"It's not crackpot, Steve. It isn't." I had to defend. "It's all, all of it, based on the word of God. It's all in the Bible, and it is the Bible gives us our design for living right. It says everything in the Bible about what is right and what is wrong."

Steve stopped what he was doing, poured himself another red wine, lit a cigarette, and squinted at me through the smoke. "Yes. Now, get me straight. I am not attacking you and your beliefs, but mister, you don't quite believe it all yourself. Certainly not the way of your father. If you did, you would never have stood up in your school and said what had to be said about the guy Messenger."

"I...er..." I gulped. "I don't quite know why I did that. Not quite."

"Shut up and listen. The Bible is a great collection of stories and a great work of art. Yes, it does give a pattern for living. But you tell me where in anything that Jesus is reported to have said—Jesus, mind, not those Old Testament hell-and-brimstone fellas—you tell me where Jesus says it's OK to bash up your wife and kids? Jesus was a cool dude. Jesus was also a kind dude. 'Do unto others as you would be done by.' Got that bugger right, didn't I?"

"Well, I guess my old man is one of the hell-and-brimstone fellas."

"Yeah. Nothing more than a stand-over bully. Probably thinks he's without sin and is itching to cast that first stone."

"You know a bit about the Bible, don't you?"

"Sweet fuck-all," said Steve, nicely. "Let's eat. God knows what it is I've cooked, but hey, look it up in your Bible if you're worried about it."

School was not easy. I faced up, fronted up, and got myself ready in my head for whatever might happen. In the end, nothing much happened. Well, nothing and everything.

While I had never been part of the in crowd—because of who I was, my background, and all that—it had always seemed as if I was in there. I am tall, reasonably fit, reasonably good to look at, and very good at all sports.

My family and background had set me apart. I had never even tasted an alcoholic drink in my life; certainly had not smoked; I didn't swear like all the other guys, or most of the girls, for that matter; and of course, I could never do anything other than go to church twice on a Sunday and to Bible study on Wednesdays. Friday nights and Saturdays I worked pumping gas. I had to work. My father had made it quite clear to me when I turned 15 that it was my duty to pay my own way! I bought my own clothes, such as they were, and had saved and saved and saved until I had enough to buy my old car...and, even then,

Arvin had helped me out a bit on that and made sure I got a good deal. So I really wasn't available for either sport teams or social life even had I wanted to be. I didn't really want to be. My ability in sport meant that I certainly had got to play in every team the school had. I had swum for the school, played rugby and soccer for the school, bashed a tennis ball for the school, and even wrestled for the school. When a school team was short of players, I got called in. I had played for every team other than, I think, girls' netball and girls' hockey. All of this meant that I had a certain protection that other nerds—and basically, I think I am one—weren't lucky enough to have.

So no one was going to bash me into the ground for my standing up for the memory of Spike Messenger. I just got completely ignored. Those who had always spoken to me stopped speaking. Those who chucked a ball round with me during breaks or lunch hour were no longer there. Guys certainly looked the other way, and many of the girls did too. I did hear "faggot," "queer," "homo," and a few other nice names flung in my direction every day for quite a while, until the name callers got sick of it. I could never spot quite where they came from or who was doing the flinging. It worried me for a couple of days, and then I just let it flow over me.

Completely ignored? Well, not quite. A new set of people, a very small set I had never noticed before, now seemed to regard me as one of their own. A bit creepy, really.

Everton is not a very liberal town. Probably no small towns, anywhere, of 15, 20 thousand people ever are. Anything or anyone the slightest bit different can generally count on being clobbered or else forced back into the acceptable mould. Everton is also a religious town. My father's Church of the New Life may be the biggest of the fundamentalist churches, but it certainly wasn't the only one. You don't see too many shops in Everton that open on a Sunday. God is big in Everton.

Even little liberal plants find it hard growing around here. We did have a refuge for battered women—until a couple of the churches said there was no need. You can guess one of those churches. A very old-fashioned community indeed. Not too many women, unless they were unmarried, worked anywhere other than in their own homes. That Spike Messenger had survived to a ripe old age of 17 in this town was a miracle indeed. Gays, men or women, are not obvious in Everton. If there have been any—other than Spike—I think they have all moved away to places where their lifestyles are more acceptable. It seems that there are now none here at all. Well, next to none.

Until the oddities at school started to creep into my line of vision, I had always thought that, with the exception of Spike, there was only one. One? Yes, one. Me.

I hated Spike Messenger. I don't know whether I hated him most because of his way-out, up-front behavior (and often, dress,) or if I hated him because he saw through me and took every opportunity to point out to me what I was and what a lie I was living. As God is my witness, a little part of me is glad that Spike is dead and I don't have to put up with his taunts ever again.

But now I can see that there are, just maybe, one or two others, and I don't think I like them any more than I liked poor, poor Spike. If I am gay, I am just about the most intolerant gay ever born. Why, for God's sake? A hangover from having it drummed into me that being gay is an offence against God's holy ordinance? Am I really an abomination in the sight of the Lord? Ah, well, if I'm doomed to hell and damnation, I'm doomed with a whole heap of others.

How do I know I am gay? Huh! Not hard to know. The sight, the smell, and the feel of only one other living person has ever made those parts of me between my legs react in a certain way and has made my heart beat so hard it near jumped out of my chest. That half-vegetable, Adrian Vanderlaar, late of Intensive Care at the Everton and Districts Hospital.

It seems abnormal that I couldn't stand the sight of both the one who spotted what I am and the one who proved to me what I am. Never in a month of Sundays could anyone accuse me of being in love with Vanderlaar. I know what the feeling is; after all, the Bible gives a lot of space to what it is. Pure, unadulterated lust. Lust! I lusted after Adrian Vanderlaar, now a vegetable. He never knew and, now, probably never will know. Thank you, God, for that small mercy.

Adrian Vanderlaar, blond Nazi, lusted after by every girl in the senior class—and me. Just how pathetic can you get?

OK, so he was a bit evil, but he wasn't all bad. He had been my science partner for over two years, and we worked closely together. Adrian wasn't a fool. He knew his good looks alone wouldn't get him through school and that I was his next best thing to insurance. I did the work. We both shared the high marks. Oh, yes, we worked closely together, and it was that closeness to him that told me in no uncertain terms what I was. I didn't mind working closely with Adrian. I drank in the sight of him, the smell of him—often beer and cigarettes even in the middle of a school day—the sound of him and the wicked stuff he could come up with and, above all, the feel of him. He only had to brush past me, lean next to me or over me, and oh, yes, it happened every time!

He could excite me just by talking his wicked stuff. Most of this stuff was about girls and what he had done to them. That was OK. Often it was about careless rabbits he had come across when he was out hunting or the neighborhood cats he had cornered and dealt to. I loved hearing about it all.

Probably, subliminally, I put myself in the place and position of the girls—or even of the unlucky bunnies or cat! Yeah, it was sick, all right. Sick through and through.

Now he's just about dead. After his accident, after Lauren's funeral, I had thought I'd like to go and see him. Then Spike Messenger got whacked, I stood up to be counted, and really, from about then on, Adrian Vanderlaar began to fade from my thinking. From what I hear, poor old near-dead Adrian now gets no visitors at all apart from his mother and father. Well, bad luck Adrian! Part of me is sensible enough to know he got no more than he deserved. While no one should have to live his life as a half-vegetable, he did bring it on himself. Silly Lauren isn't living any life at all.

CHAPTER SIX

Reckon now, I had become doomed to the fires of hell anyway. Certainly never did anything wicked with Vanderlaar, but the thought had certainly lived in my mind...and other places! That all leads to the same unenviable fate. God, I was even a drinker! Living with Steve Peterson for a while, it was inevitable. The days turned into weeks and the weeks into months. Time slipped by so quickly, so comfortably.

"Look, man, even Jesus was all for a drink now and then. What about the wedding where he got to work on the water and turned it into wine?"

"That story is illustrative only," I instructed him. "Bible scholars reckon it wasn't wine at all. Certainly it wasn't intoxicating. Unfermented grape juice is what it was."

"Oh, I see," said Steve, smiling, those wicked deep-blue eyes of his twinkling. "Even though it says wine, it really should be read as unfermented grape juice; and Jesus turned the water into unfermented grape juice. That what you're saying?" Very sweetly.

I got suckered in. "Something like that."

"Crap," said Steve, politely. "Two things, mate, spring to my mind. First off, Jesus and the guys he hung with were not the sort of dudes who turned up at a wedding and said 'Please give me a glass of unfermented fruit juice.' Wine means wine, and wine meant wine even back a couple of thousand years. Those guys were living, breathing men who would've enjoyed a drink as much as any other living, breathing man."

"If you say so," I said. "What was the second thing?"

"You're so damn hot on what is said of the Bible being the literal word of God and all that, and man shouldn't be tinkering with it or interpreting it to suit themselves; e.g., mister, your buddy Spike likely spilling his seed in all the wrong places and being condemned to the fires of hell for eternity."

"Yes, he will be. So?"

"And now here you are telling me that your lot are quite happy to interpret wine into unfermented grape juice just to suit yourselves. Gotcha!" And he smiled broadly.

I sighed. "It's no use talking to people like you about it. Bible scholars are pretty clever guys and they know what they're talking about. You can take their word."

"Pull the other one, kid. It's not their word...oh, to hell with it." He walked to the fridge and took out a beer, opened it, and handed it to me. "Come on, Bozo, try one. You might find you'll like it, and I'll bet my last dollar the skies won't open, the finger of the Lord won't poke down from heaven and nail you. Go on," he dared me.

Why not? I was beyond redemption anyway. Other things had begun to gnaw at my thinking. Here was this guy who had a drink or two most days—and sometimes more. He lived a good honest life, and even more important, he had held out a hand to me when I needed some help...was the finger of the Lord, as he put it, poised to nail this man because he enjoyed a few glasses of wine? I took the beer.

I enjoyed that beer. I remember that much. I think I enjoyed the next beer just as much. I can't quite remember the third one or the...

The next morning when I woke up I knew I was never going to drink, not ever again, no matter what the temptation, no matter what devil tried to force it on me.

Later that day, feeling quite a lot better, I did have another beer. But only just the one. One beer isn't such a bad thing and can really be very refreshing.

Down the purple path! I took the next couple of steps myself. I wasn't going to be goaded into them by Steven Peterson, with his ever-present grin and smooth-talking ways and to whom I seemed to be feeling increasingly close.

There were always half-used packs of cigarettes scattered around Steve's house. When I was at home and he wasn't, I used up a couple of them and became a smoker. It took a bit of effort, more than a few coughing fits, and for just a little while, the odd bout of dizziness. Common sense tells me that I am lucky that I will never become the most enthusiastic smoker, and at least at this very early stage in my smoking career I can give up the wicked, hazardous habit. But I became smoker enough to wipe the grin off Steve Peterson's face.

He opened up my by-now nightly beer and handed it to me and began to pat his pockets in the way I was now used to. This time I grinned at him. "Here, have one of mine." I whipped out a pack of cigarettes and offered it to him. He blinked, took one, I lit it for him with my lighter, then lit one for myself and blew a good cloud of smoke up towards the ceiling.

"Jesus!" said Steve.

"Listen, mate," and I went on grinning, taking another drag on my cigarette, "a guy can't enjoy a beer without a fuckin' smoke!" And then I got exactly what I deserved. I choked and know full well that I blushed beetroot red.

It seemed about an hour later that Steve stopped rolling around on the floor laughing. "Look, mister, right now I should power into a good long lecture about stupid habits, but I'm the last one to talk. You want to smoke, you smoke. That's your

PEBBLE IN A POOL

decision. I gave you a beer a couple of weeks back because, you poor little sod, you seemed to be so screwed up, uptight, the weight of the whole damn world on your shoulders, and right or wrong, it seemed to me that the occasional drink might help to relax you. Might have seemed I was daring you to do it, but I wasn't." He didn't give me his wicked grin but just an ordinary smile. "Hey..."

"What?"

"You don't have to prove anything to me. You don't have to prove to me that you're a man. You are. Every good-lookin' inch of you! You proved that to me back...you know when," and he looked very serious. "Believe me, man, I am the last person you have to prove anything to. Drink, smoke, swear if you want, it's your business. But you don't have to do it for me."

"Good-looking, you reckon?" I smiled at him.

"God help me! You are only 17! Yes, you look OK. Very OK. Be better with a decent haircut and a few new clothes."

"That's cool," I said. "Except I can't afford any of that stuff."

"Don't worry," said Steve. "I'd already decided to treat you— for your birthday. You know, just to help the stud part of you shine through."

"Very cool," I didn't argue. I finished my beer and had another cigarette.

CHAPTER SEVEN

Life was not all sweetness and light.

Arvin Singh's gas station is not in the best part of town. Nothing wrong with where it is, but it is simply not your upmarket sort of place. It is on the edge of Everton's small industrial area and is the nearest gas station to the three main industrial plants—a large timber mill, a chicken processing plant, and a small meat works. Arvin does very good business indeed. The trucks that serve the three plants all use our gas station—generally, after they have dropped off logs, chickens, and livestock. Equally important, the workers from the three plants, mostly men but a few women, all call in at Arvin's for gas, drinks, cigarettes, and whatever food they can find. Most of them are a cheerful lot, use language a bit like Steve's, spend quite a bit, and are never any trouble. Arvin keeps the place open late because the three factories work in shifts. People from the residential parts of the town don't often need to go out of their way to top up at Arvin's, but sometimes they do for one reason or another.

Ten P.M., and I was about to close the place one Friday night after I had been living at Steve's for a couple of months. It was a cold and dark night. The ever-present rain had stopped for a while, but everything sure was bleak and uninviting. I had stowed away most of the outside junk inside, display boards and stuff like that, when the old car rolled in and stopped by the pumps. My heart sank; I tried to ignore the vehicle and its load, and concentrated, for as long as possible, on carrying a couple of crates of motor oil into the shop part of the station. I wasn't allowed to ignore it for too long.

"Come on, ya fuckin' homo, we want us some service!"

It was Snout Hogg and two of his bully-boy buddies, Lump and Bazza. They were all about my age, and these three and a couple of others had terrorized Everton High until one by one they had dropped out over the last year or so. A nasty lot indeed. Like bullies everywhere, they tended to work in a pack, picking off the small, the weak, and the unwary. Because I had never been small, weak, or unwary, they had never given me much trouble. Clearly this was about to change! Here I was, all alone. There were three of them and they were hungry for a spot of fun and there was no one at all around to prevent them having it.

"Come on, ya dirty bumfuck, get over here," yelled Snout, a nasty smirk across his spotty pig face. "But don't ya come too close. Us guys don' want ya fuckin' AIDS. Fill 'er up," and he rolled his window right down.

"Look at 'im," and Bazza leaned out a rear window. "Fuckin' fags make ya wanna puke," and he spat. For some unknown reason Bazza and Lump sat together in the backseat, Snout alone up front.

I should have just filled the tank and trusted to luck that would see them on their way. I didn't. I guess I was six or eight feet from the car when I said, "You're not getting any gas until you turn off the engine and all stop smoking. It says there." I pointed to the sign. "It's a danger."

"Hear that, guys?" and Snout mimicked me. "It's a danger. It's a danger. Come on, guys, let's show the dirty poof what a real danger is." He leaned over and, I think, went to grope for something on the floor of the car under the passenger-side seat.

"Aw, geez, Snout," Lump spoke. "Shit, man, let's jus' get the fuckin' gas..."

And then I wasn't alone! From the shadows at the side of the building Steve Peterson materialized, sleek, silent, and somehow deadly. "What seems to be the problem, gentlemen?" He spoke quite softly and there was the faintest trace of a smile on his lips, but I could see now in the light of the forecourt that there was no matching smile in his eyes. With absolutely effortless ease he leaned in at the front window, grabbed Snout's nearest arm with one hand, then Snout's lit cigarette in the fingers of his other hand. He took a deep drag on the cigarette, blew smoke directly into Snout's face, and as he blew on the lighted tip, he said, "Unscrew the tank cap, Paul. We'll just slip this in and show these guys what a great danger smoking can be!"

There was a startled squawk from the backseat as Steve went on talking without raising his voice. "Well, maybe not. Don't want the innocent fried as well, do we?" Laughing, he stubbed out Snout's smoke.

Snout found his voice. "Wha' the fuck? You ain't the bloody curry muncher. Who the—" But he wasn't quite given the time to finish his question.

"Manners, my man. Manners!" Steve was now smiling broadly. Snout had somehow managed to get the window almost half closed, leaving a gap of an inch or so between door frame and glass. It was into this gap that Steve now forced Snout's arm. Snout screamed as Steve said, pleasantly, "Ouch! Oh, I bet that hurt!" Then he directed his attention towards the occupants of the backseat, who were clearly on the point of leaving their mate to a fate they did not feel like sharing. "No, guys. Don't move. Just stay where you are. We've not finished here yet. Just wait patiently, you'll get your turn." Spoken softly, almost sweetly as he bent Snout's arm quite cruelly, generating another agonized scream. There was something about his voice that kept the other two frozen, now quite still. They really could have escaped. "Good boys," Steve smiled in at them.

Snout gathered one or two of his fevered wits and with his free hand attempted to put the still-running car into gear, revving the engine for some sort of getaway.

"Tsk tsk tsk tsk," and Steve really did make the sound. "You've got to be quicker than that, fella." Absolutely effortlessly, he leaned in at the window, killed the engine, and slipped out the keys. Then he worked on Snout's arm again with wonderfully loud results.

Lump found a little bit of voice. "You can't do that, mate. Ya hurtin' him real bad. Shit," and he dug Bazza in the ribs. "Get out, man. Get in there and ring the cops."

But Bazza was frozen, freezing a little bit more as Steve said, "Stay where you are, both of you. But a good idea. Paul, get inside and phone the cops, would you?"

"No no no no no, please not the cops." Snout stopped squealing long enough to find his voice, a look of sheer terror in his eyes. I couldn't tell whether the terror resulted from the pain he was feeling or the prospect of the police arriving.

"All right," said Steve, purring. "We'll keep the police out of it for now, although believe me, it would prove much less physically painful for you in the long run if you would let us call them. Mind you, judging by the state of this vehicle, I'm not surprised you don't want them snooping around. Tsk tsk." That sound again. "In quite a derelict state, isn't it? Quite unsafe on the roads if you ask me. Just as well I'm holding the keys," and he chuckled.

By now none of the three were into disagreeing with Steve Peterson. Had I been any of them, I wouldn't have either! Here he was, Steve, really one against three—I wasn't counting myself at this stage—and with next to no effort at all, he had them fully terrified and as mesmerized as a nighttime rabbit facing the headlights of an oncoming car. So far, apart from dealing to Snout's one arm quite painfully, he had done nothing at all, had not even raised his voice. I was as mesmerized as the others.

That's only part of the truth. I was both mesmerized and getting very excited in a way that none of the others would have been! Excited, oh, yes, and also fully enjoying the sight and sound of these three getting back just a little bit of what had been their own treatment of others for so many years. This was fun! I wanted it to continue. I wanted these sods to suffer. They did. Something told me that Steven Peterson was also enjoying himself. He was so smoothly, gracefully lethal. He seemed comfortable in what he was doing and one thousand percent in control.

Snout found a bit more voice. "Look, mate, didn't mean no trouble or nuthin'. Giz me keys and we'll fuck off. Don' need no gas after all."

"No, Snowdrop, you don't. This motor vehicle is in far too unsafe a condition for you to drive and risk your valuable life and those of your lady friends in the back or, more important, other decent people who may be using our roads. I would be failing in my duty if I let you. You won't be needing horsepower. Marigold and Fatboy back there will be pushing. Manpower, if you could call it that." Steve jiggled Snout's keys in front of his captive's eyes before heaving them as far as he could into the darkness and a patch of scrub on the far side of the road. There was a low and agonized groan from Snout. "Now, first things first, er...gentlemen. I require a deep and abject apology from each of you for your rudeness to my friend, Paul, here. You first, Snowdrop." Another little prompt to Snout's trapped arm.

"E-e-e-chh...ug, er, sorry..."

"I am very sorry, Mr. Carter. I am positive those are the words you're groping for," Steve said with the sweetest of smiles.

I have to admit, there was a broad and unsweet smile on my face and a warm glow everywhere else as each of the three slugs gritted out their full apologies to Mr. Carter.

"A kindly word of warning to each of you," said Steve. "Should you come around here again, or even if I see any of you or hear of any plans your birdlike brains may be harboring of sweet revenge...if you breathe anywhere near me, or him..." Steve nodded towards me. "...should I hear of you harming any other living creature, even a mouse or a blowfly," chuckle chuckle, "rest assured, I'll get you, and then I'll really deal to you. I love this work, and I'll be itching to get really stuck in. None of this gentle shit next time! Geddit?"

They got it.

"Now, Fatboy and Marigold, when I give you the word, and not before, you get out and start pushing." Steve beckoned me towards him and spoke very softly. "Take the bastard on the far side. Just do exactly what you see me do. You can do it," and then he turned back to Snout. "As a friendly reminder that I keep my word." He smiled. "And just to help you get rid of any little thoughts you may have of escape when I release your arm, here's a little extra something," and Steve took the middle finger of Snout's hand. I heard the crack. I don't know whether he broke it or dislocated it, and I don't really care. Snout Hogg screamed louder than a pig being stuck.

I moved to the other side of the car and waited for Lump to get out, keeping an eye on Steve. I was not worried that I would fail to follow whatever it was Steve had in store. I had never been a world-beating wrestler, but I sure knew the moves.

Lump and Bazza were, understandably, not too keen on getting out. "Come on, guys," Steve urged. "Haven't got all night."

And he helped Bazza out of the car, spun him round, put a choker hold round his neck, and forced one arm up his back hard. There was some squawking but no defense. I obliged with Lump. Flabby, no resistance, unless you could call terrified trembling a sort of resistance. Lump was like a jelly. "You guys have got off far too lightly compared to your mate there." Releasing Bazza's arm, he grabbed his long and greasy hair and bopped his head very hard down onto the top of the car. Then for good measure he bopped it another couple of times. Then he let go, and Bazza staggered just a bit. "Start pushing, mate."

It felt great to give precisely the same treatment to Lump, but I was clearly not as practiced as Steve at bopping. Either that, or because Lump was born with a thin skull, I just about knocked him out, and it took Steve some time to encourage him to stop staggering dazed and dizzy and to put his shoulder to the car and start pushing. "Good night, gentlemen. Thanks for your business," Steve called out as the car rolled slowly from the forecourt, out onto the deserted road and, picking up a little speed, down the slight hill away from the gas station.

I followed Steve inside into the staff room. He leaned against the wall. He was shaking and he kept his eyes downcast and away from me. He lit a cigarette and smoked for a moment. Then he slumped down in a seat and dragged a hand through his hair. "Oh, fuck," he said, softly. "Oh, fuck."

I was trembling, too. Shaking all over with an excitement that was...what? Adrenaline? I gulped and moved towards Steve where he sat. I put out a hand to touch his shoulder. "What's—"

"Don't touch me." He reacted as if he had received an electric shock.

I moved back, a little hurt. Then he stood. "Sorry," he muttered. He looked me up and down, smiling slightly. "You too, eh?"

"What?"

Steve seemed to pull himself together. "Nothing. Nothing at all." Almost a snap, but he did continue to smile. "Come on. I'll help you close stuff down, whatever you have to do. Then we'll bugger off home and get something to eat. Follow me closely. Not that I think those suckers will be waiting, not ever..." He turned in the doorway, looked at me, and said, "Violence isn't an answer to anything, man. You know that. It's just that, well, sometimes, with rats like that, it seems the only language they understand."

"Yeah, I know. Hey, but it was sure cool, eh?"

"No!" He raised his voice. "It wasn't cool. I got fuckin' carried away."

"Where did you learn—"

He didn't give me a chance. "Shut up and close up. Let's go home."

I guess I got home about 10 minutes after Steve. His truck drives a lot more quickly than my old car allows me to. He was on the phone, and I heard him say, "I think it would pay...yeah, a very close check. Just a hunch...thanks, Joe. Bye." And he put down the receiver.

"Who was that?" I asked, shrugging out of my jacket.

"No one. Just a wrong number," he lied. "Heat up that fried rice, man. Stuff we had last night. Three minutes nuked should do it. I'll feed Audrey and Mr. Cat."

It was as if nothing had happened.

CHAPTER EIGHT

The good old Everton grapevine never fails. Only God knows how it works, and He's not divulging! Snout, Bazza, Lump, Steve, and me—a friendly private gathering late one night at a deserted gas station, not another soul within sight or earshot, and yes, yet again the whole world knows. Not quite accurately, of course. After all, Snout Hogg had not had both legs broken and Bazza had not lost half his head of greasy hair and I think Lump still has both ears, even if there isn't much between them. I guess the three of them could have met up with someone else over the weekend, but that did seem doubtful.

Monday morning. School. Pariah to hero in no time flat! I wouldn't have a bit of it! Not one little bit! Pride may well be a deadly sin, but I don't give a shit! I was proud of myself and how I reacted.

Morning break. Three, four of the guys who had previously, a lifetime ago it now seemed, been friendly acquaintances sort of sidled up, grinning. They were throwing a ball between them. "Come on, Carter," one of them called out. "Throw a few passes?"

I looked at the three of them and they waited, sort of expectantly. I gave a smile that Steve would have been proud of and said, politely, "Fuck off." Then I walked off to sit in the spring sun, just a little bit closer to the small group of weirdos who weren't weirdos to me anymore but were the only people who had given me the time of day for quite some long time.

"Heard what you did to Snout Hogg, Paul," said one of them, moving to sit a little bit closer. "That must've been so cool."

"Violence isn't an answer to anything, man," I said. "You know that."

"Yeah, right!" said the guy.

"It really isn't, Derek," I said, using his name for the very first time.

"Just wish I had been there," said Derek, with great feeling, as he smiled at me.

I smiled back at him.

I eased up at school. I had no worries academically and knew that even with slightly less effort my marks would be enough, more than enough, for whatever came later. This was the problem: What was going to come later? I had no idea. I had thought of engineering, thought of law, even thought of medicine. None of them really appealed. Thought too of the army, the navy, the air force. Teaching? Surely I should have had some idea by now, but truthfully, I hadn't. The best idea would probably be to simply finish high school and then work for a year or two and get enough money behind me so that I could afford to do whatever it was I didn't know I wanted to do!

My bank account was growing quite splendidly thanks to Arvin and, of course, to Steve. I worked all day Sundays for Arvin, and so far, God's long finger hadn't come down to skewer me for the sin. He was probably saving up and adding Sunday work to my nightly beer, the odd smoke, and God help me, even occasionally taking His name in vain! A growing list.

"What's this?" Steve pointed to a box sitting just to the side of the front door.

"How on earth would I know?" We had just both got home late afternoon, early evening.

"Hey! It's a pie." He had opened up the box. "Who the hell..."

I looked at it. I knew. I recognized the dish and recognized the sort of pie. I had eaten plenty of these meat pies. "Give it to old Audrey, Mr. Cat, whoever. Chuck it out." I walked inside.

Steve followed me. "Your mother?"

"Yes," I said shortly. "Who else? None of the others. Certainly not him. Only thing he knows about bloody pies is how to shove them in his fat gob and swallow."

"Simmer down."

"I'm not simmered up."

"Yeah? From what you've told me, it must have taken your mother every tiny little ounce of her courage to bring this pie out here and leave it for you. You know the risks she would have taken. Seems to me she must be just about as brave as you."

I looked at him for a moment and then sat down and went on looking as my eyes filled up. Bugger it! I saw her as I had last seen her, pathetic little thing trying in a teeny-tiny and useless way to stop him doing what he was doing to me. "All right. We'll eat the fuckin' thing. I don't hate my mother. I don't hate my mother. No, I don't..."

"Hey. It's OK, man. It's OK."

"No, it's not OK. I can't help her. I can't do anything for her. Besides, it's not as if she wants any help anyway. She...oh, I dunno."

"Well, who does know? I didn't have a mother, so how the hell would I know," said Steve. For the first time ever he told me something about himself. But he left it at that.

We ate the pie and I washed the pie dish, put it back in its box, did up the box the way it had been. Then I undid the box, got a scrap of paper and pen, and wrote a note, a very short note. "Thank you" was all it said. Then I put the box out by the front door and, sure enough, after about a week the box was replaced, and Steve and I got a chocolate cake to munch through.

Nothing much happened for a little while, except that the weather started to warm up, the lawns around Steve's house started to grow again, flowers came out, and trees came into leaf.

Then a lot happened—very, very quickly.

Adrian Vanderlaar got out of hospital.

Snout Hogg, Bazza, Lump, and one other guy were said to be spending a great deal of time, either together or singly, down at the cop shop, and Snout Hogg's car had been impounded and taken apart for forensic testing.

I turned 18. Yes, the big one-eight! I could now vote, go to the pub or a bar and buy a drink, buy cigarettes legally, fight and die for my country, and run up debts on credit cards I didn't have. It felt good.

Adrian Vanderlaar stopped being a vegetable and surfaced, struggling back to a semblance of life. He looked the same and sounded the same, but he certainly wasn't the same. He came back to school and discovered what being a pariah felt like. It wasn't so much the guys who shunned him; it was his previous lifeblood, the girls. He was no use to the guys either, and soon they just ignored him. Adrian was now a paraplegic, useless from the waist down. He didn't drive a car anymore; he drove a wheelchair.

All of a sudden I found that I actually liked him as a person. One thing cannot be denied about Adrian: Two legs or no legs, he can certainly be entertaining. I had no problem facing him at all. I certainly didn't lust after him...not one little bit of me, oh, thank you, God!

"Heard all about you, Carter, and what you did. Fuck, if I'd been around when you did it, I'd have sure given you shit."

"Yeah?" At least he was honest.

"But you're OK. Reckon you did the right thing."

"How'd you work that out?" I asked. "Why should it be the right thing and OK with you now?"

"Had time to think, eh. Look at me. I whacked someone I actually liked and who didn't deserve any bit of what she got. You? You stood up for someone I don't think you ever liked very much. No one liked old Spike. I sure gave him hell. But he got whacked for being no more than what he was and always had been. That's not fair. Geddit?"

"Not really. But thanks for saying it. D'you need a push?"

"No. I don't need a fuckin' push. I gotta do this for myself...but you can open the door." He looked up at me. "I've gotta pay, you know, for what I've done."

"I can see that."

"Didn't mean that. I gotta pay for killing Lauren. I'm gonna be charged. Probably manslaughter. I'll go to jail. Fair enough, I reckon." Then he grinned. "Hope they got a jail takes wheelchairs." He went on grinning. "Least I'll be safe from what they reckon happens to young guys sent to jail."

"Wha...oh, that! You still got a dirty mind, Adrian."

"Too right, I have. Not that it'll do me much good." This time he did sound slightly bitter. "You still workin' for old Singh down Eastside?"

"Why?"

"Thought I'd roll by there occasionally for a chat. You can't be busy all the time."

I looked very hard at him. "No, we're not. Yeah, fine. If you feel like it."

"I've got to master this bastard." He patted his chair. "And I will. It's not going stop me from doin' things."

It's a very strange world where someone like Adrian

Vanderlaar can be so much better and more human as a cripple than he ever was as a whole person.

I bumped into Lump Manning just after I came out of the town library, where I had been looking for a book the school didn't have. The town library didn't have it either. Bumping into Lump was a glorious moment for me. He gulped, opened and closed his mouth, opened it again, looking for all the world like a goldfish facing a shark. I couldn't help it—I grinned.

"Gidday, Lump," I greeted him. "Howzit hangin'?"

A look of sheer terror spread across his face. He opened his mouth one final time and out came a sort of squawk. His eyes wide open, he turned on his heel and ran away from me down the street. What made the whole thing truly beautiful was that he turned one last time to look back at me, still horror-stricken. Then the idiot ran into a sandwich board on the footpath and fell over flat on his face. Sometimes life can be so sweet! I wonder if I will ever be a Christian again!

Chapter Nine

The evening before my birthday Steve and I were watching the news on television. There was a knock, a very quiet knock, on the door. Steve opened it. "Paul," he called over his shoulder. "There's someone to see you."

It was my mother. All sorts of feelings ran through me as I stood behind Steve in the open doorway.

"Mrs. Carter?" Steve held out a hand and my mother took it. "Please come in. I've er...got one or two things that need doing outside. I'll just leave you two together."

"There's no need, Steve," I said. But he had gone.

"These are for you, dear," said my mother. "For tomorrow. It's just a pair of socks and a cake." She spoke in a voice just a degree above a whisper. "I had better go now." In spite of her words she stayed at the door.

I looked down at her. She stood small and silent in her plain overcoat. Her straggly, fairish hair was drawn tight into a bun on the nape of her neck. I couldn't hate her. I couldn't. I couldn't hate this poor little brainwashed woman who, 18 years ago tomorrow, had given birth to me.

"Please come in, Mum," I said as I took her arm. "Thank you for the cakes and stuff."

"Little man" was all she said. Then she began to cry, and so did I.

Howling, I said, "I am not bad, Mum. I am not evil, Mum. I

am not going to hell and God does not hate me. I've done nothing wrong and I never did. I only did what I thought was right."

She led me towards the sofa and we sat next to each other. She did her best to comfort me, and I did the same for her. "There, now," she said. "No more. You're a big boy now." She managed a tight little smile.

"Big boys can cry," I sniffed.

"So I see. I...I've..." she tried to start.

"It doesn't matter, Mum. Does he know you're here?" I didn't wait for her to answer. "No, of course he doesn't. You shouldn't have come."

"Your father is away this week. It's conference time."

"What about Danny and Hannah?"

"They're fine. I feel sure they would have sent you their—"

"No. Mum. Don't try. They wouldn't, and you know it."

"Danny has a school camp this week and I've let Hannah stay overnight with one of her friends."

"How convenient," I said. "He'd kick you out too if he knew you were here. You better be careful none of the congregation spots you. You'd be in all sorts of trouble."

"You should not think ill of your father, Paul. He is your father. He took what action he thought was right and was for your own good."

There was a limit to how much I could take. "No, Mother. No, don't give me that stuff. I did nothing wrong to him or you or me. You got no need to preach at me. Honor thy father and thy mother? OK, Mum, I'll honor you, but not him. I'm not his son anymore. He said that. He did. You heard him."

"Don't be so angry, son. We all say things. We do things in the heat of the moment that, later, we may regret."

"Yes, Mother. I know all that. Something tells me, though, that he's certainly not regretting anything he's done. Let's leave it." I looked into her eyes. "Has he hit you lately?" She didn't answer me. Instead, she lowered her eyes and played at the small, screwed-up handkerchief in her fingers. "Hit you lately, has he?" I asked.

"Your father does not hit me," she whispered. "You have no right to question your father's—"

"He hits you, Mum. He hits you."

"Any chastisement meted out by your father to me is the business, solely, of your father and me. Anything that your father does is done from love. It is not for you or for me to question his actions." She got to her feet. "I must go now."

Steve came back in from wherever he had been. "Surely not leaving so soon, Mrs. Carter. How about a cup of coffee?" He nodded towards one of the boxes my mother had brought. "Any chance of one of those great chocolate cakes being in there?" He gave her a stunning smile. "Better have at least a coffee with us to celebrate your son's big day tomorrow."

My mother stayed for a further 15 minutes and did her best to enjoy a hurried coffee and cake. Conversation was not easy. Not that there was tension in the air—rather, there was nothing.

I took her out to her car, gave her a hug, and kissed the top of her head. "Be careful, Mother," I whispered.

"You be careful, Paul. I pray for you. You are a good boy..." She looked up at me and gave a little smile. "There now," she added. "You will always be my son," she said as she stroked my cheek.

I waved her goodbye and watched as she drove down the driveway and out onto the winding road back into town. I hoped and prayed that she really would be careful. Feeling empty, I walked back inside the house.

"OK?" Steve enquired.

"Yep," I replied.

"Liar," said Steve, getting up and moving to a small cabinet. "You make more coffee and I'll drag out the whisky. Nothing like a slug of whisky in a coffee on a cool night. Besides, you're old enough now...or will be in a few hours! Have one?" He waved the bottle.

"Fuckin' great," I said. "Give me two of 'em."

"Learn to walk before you try to run, kid. Take the word of someone who knows. Families, huh!"

I carried the coffee pot over to the table and we both sat. "Seems to me we can both do without them. Why don't you ever say anything about yours? You never do."

"There's nothing much to tell," said Steve.

"I don't want to be nosy." I looked at him.

He smiled at me. "Oh, yes you do! I told you, my mother died when I was very little. I was 2. I have no memory of her. I had—have—a father and two much older brothers. I was shunted off to live with my grandmother. She brought me up when I was a little nipper. I loved her. When I was 7 I was sent away to boarding school and, during all those years, I spent all my holidays, vacations with my grandmother."

"Didn't you ever see your father and brothers?"

"From time to time. Not often. He and my brothers had their lives and, I guess, I had mine. Didn't really ever cross my mind there was anything strange about it. I even enjoyed being away at school. I was a tough little bastard and always one of the guys."

I looked at him. I believed him! A king among boys—and men! I could see him as one of the top guys, lording it over all the lesser mortals. Some are born to rule and others are born to be ruled. Steve Peterson was well and truly in the first group.

"The first drop of rain in my life was when Granny died. I was the same age as you'll be in an hour or two. I still miss the old dame." He poured another slug of whisky into his coffee and lit a cigarette. "It was then, as they say, the shit hit the fan, familywise."

"I'm sorry. I don't want to pry."

He grinned at me. "Yeah, right! You want to know it all. Granny left everything she owned to me. It wasn't a great fortune—just her house, a few valuable odds and ends, and a few thousand dollars."

"That was nice of her."

"Huh! Well, yes it was. My old man had been her only child. He sued for her estate. Well, he sued me, didn't he? His own kid! She must have known he would, because she had left everything so watertight he couldn't do a bloody thing. He lost. I got everything. I think I've only seen him once or twice since. It's not as if he needed her few bits and pieces. He was, is, as rich as Croesus himself. Big-shot lawyer. My two brothers are his partners. They could buy and sell me a thousand times over." Steve took a deep drag on his cigarette and blew three perfect smoke rings, an ability I envied. "So, man, there you have it."

"What did you do after you left school? You haven't been around here, around Everton, for all that long."

"The usual. Bummed around. Bit of study. Travelled a bit. That's about it." Steve smiled at me again.

"I bet there's more to it than that."

"You really do have to know it all, don't you?" And he went on smiling.

"Well...you know all about me. My life is an open book."

"Is it?" Steve's eyes narrowed, and he looked closely at me. "I know precisely what you want me to know. You're the same as everyone else. No exception. There's more to anyone than meets the eye—you included!"

"Rot! Anyway, then you came here."

"You've got it. I used Granny's money to buy this place, set up my workshop...and the rest is history, as they say." He pulled himself to his feet, walked across to a cabinet and opened a drawer, fossicked around. "Here. This is my favorite shot of Granny and me. I think I was about 14, 15." He laughed. "And 'shot' really is the right word!"

What a photo! "Wow! She must have been a tough old lady."

"Taught me just about everything I know, oh, about life... whatever." He looked over my shoulder and into the picture. "Fuck, that was a great day."

"Not for those ducks," I said, looking at the picture of a very tough old lady and a beautiful, wild-looking, grinning boy, each holding shotguns and standing behind a mountain of dead ducks. It also showed that Steve Peterson started smoking at a very young age. Granny had set a bad example.

"Yeah. She could be pretty lethal on various forms of wildlife, but she certainly loved people. I guess that's why I came here and had a go at using her money to help others. Stuffed up on that one, as you know full well."

"I don't understand."

"She taught me a great lesson. If anyone has got less than you, is in need—if you can help, you help them. Any collector who came to her door, providing she didn't think they were a crook, she gave. She always gave folding money. Guess a little bit of it rubbed off on me. More coffee?" Without waiting for my reply, he topped my cup and followed up with another slug of whisky. "Had no time for what she called Jesus freaks. I'm afraid she would have given your old man the bum's rush—probably with the action end of her shotgun!"

"Good on her," I said, with great feeling. "But you are doing OK here, Steve."

"Not in quite the way I intended. Oh, yes," he grinned. "I'm doing very nicely. You know that. You do my books."

"So?"

"When I came here, it was with the object in mind of doing something useful. Always been good with my hands, pottering around with carpentry and all that shit. Loved it. I was going to buy up old, broken-down stuff, renovate, restore it, and sell it off cheap to people who couldn't afford much. Nice idea. But, when you think about it, helluva patronizing. I found out in next to no time that poor people would far rather have new stuff and put themselves in hock to the big-store buggers in order to get it."

"I know you don't sell off anything you make very cheaply. Not even half cheaply. You charge an arm and a leg. That table last week..."

"I know," he laughed. "Started off cheap, and I thought I was achieving what I set out to do. Everything I did up sold like hot-cakes. Then one day I was up in the city, scouting around for more old broken shit, and I was looking around this trendy, pseudoantique decorator outfit...you'll never guess what I found."

"Tell me." I took another slurp of my coffee. There's something cool about coffee with a slug of whisky in it. I felt warm all over.

"There, right in front of me, was the table and chairs I had sold off for a song a few weeks earlier. The price label on it was exactly 20 times what I had charged for it! The rest is history." Steve laughed out loud. "Bugger the poor!"

"Well, I think it's great."

"Oh, yes you would, you right-wing little capitalist shit. Screw the other bastard before he screws you! So much for Jesus and what He preached."

"You know I am not like that at all. OK, I'm glad you make a lot from what you do, but I also know the time you spend on each piece, and if rich customers want to pay, that is all right."

"Yeah, man, I know you're not like that, otherwise you wouldn't be living here. Here..." he said. He fished in the pocket of his jacket and he handed me an envelope. "Happy birthday."

"It's not my birthday yet. Another hour."

"Don't split hairs. Open the bloody thing."

There was a card. Very simple. Just one flower on the front and no printed message. Steve had written inside the card, "Happy Birthday, Paul. My home will always be your home. Love, Steve." Then I read the check he had included: $500!

"I can't take this." My hand trembled. I looked at him.

"It's only money," he said.

"It's a lot of money. You can't—"

"Afford it? Pull the other one, man! Listen, you stupid little prick, I told you I was going to give you a few decent clothes to wear and the first good haircut of your life."

"Yes."

He nodded down towards the check I was clutching in my hand. "If there's not enough there, I'll top it up. OK?" And he stood.

"Thank you. Thank you very much for everything," I turned to him and gave him a hug. I felt him tremble, shiver slightly.

Steve returned my hug and then gently pushed me away. "I've jacked it up with Arvin. He's giving you Saturday off. We'll go up to the city and have a bit of a spend-up. God knows, you need more than one pair of jeans."

"I've got two pairs," I said indignantly.

"You've probably got one-and-a-half pairs," said Steve. "Most of your other pair seems to be missing. As for a decent jacket...oh, what the hell. Let's have a day of spending. I feel like it. Indulge an old man."

"I'd hardly call you that! An old man?" I said.

"There are times when you make me feel like one," said Steve. "Now get off to bed."

I puddled around, tidied up the place a bit, showered, cleaned teeth, and after a while, walked through the sitting room again on my way to bed. Steve still sat there. He had propped up the beautiful photograph of his grandmother, himself, and the heap of ducks and was staring at it, muttering. He did not seem very happy, and I think he was slightly drunk. The level of the whisky in the bottle was low.

It is not only feathers that make fine birds, goes the old saying. I'm not sure that's right. I had the greatest shopping trip of my life and scored a bundle of fine feathers. Now I want to wear them all the time!

I had no idea that a haircut cost a small fortune. I had only ever had my hair cut in our kitchen by my mother. I have now learnt that my mother is not one of the world's better hair-cutters.

Looks have never meant much to me, or so I told myself. But is this a lie? Maybe so. Although I am not bad to look at, I have never thought of myself as good-looking. Just ordinary. My ears are set close to my head, and I've got a good mop of straight dirty-blond hair.

"Hmmm," said Mavis the hairdresser, holding half of my hair in one hand. "I think we can do something with this, Steve."

That was all well and good, except it wasn't Steve's hair. Mavis seemed to be a friend of Steve's. "I just want a tidy-up sort of thing, trim thing..." I said.

"Is that right, dear?" I don't think Mavis was listening. "I'd give my right arm for a mop like this." She waved a dangerous-looking pair of scissors perilously close to one of my ears. I had a feeling she was going to get most of my hair anyway.

"Transform him, Mave," said Steve. "The world's your oyster."

"Pity he hadn't been here last week for the competitions. Could have done with a model like this. I won, you know."

"I know, Mave," said Steve. "Read it in the paper. Nice pic. Well done. Can I smoke in here?"

"You know perfectly well you can't," said Mavis, poking and prodding my head. She didn't register me in her thinking as a real-life person. I was just a head of hair waiting to be massacred. I needed a cigarette! "Pour us a coffee, love," Mavis ordered Steve. "Maybe little er...whatsit, Peter here—"

"Paul," I got a word in edgewise.

"Whatever," said Mavis, and settled to work.

Mavis, I now realize, is a true hair artist. Snip snip snip and clip clip clip and I ended up a different person. My scalp had been massaged, shampooed, creamed with some sort of gunk, and she had got to work with her blowtorch drier thing and turned me into what I am today—an almost-hunk. From now on, no matter how much it costs, I am going to take my head of spectacular hair to a proper hairdresser. Enough said.

Steve had a haircut too. Steve looked much the same after his haircut as he had before. After Mavis extracted her small fortune from us both, we went off shopping for clothes.

It may not only be fine feathers that make fine birds, but they sure as hell help. If I thought that Mavis charged a small fortune, I soon found out that fine feathers cost even more. By the end of the shopping spree, the $500, a fortune in itself, did need a little bit of topping up. However, I did the topping—Steve had done enough.

Steve looked me up and down. "You pay for dressing, man. You surely do. You're not fool enough to think that any of this crap can make you a better person, but I'd be a liar if I didn't say you look good."

"Cool," I said, admiring myself in a mirror. "What d'you reckon? The dark blue or the grey?"

"Dark blue," said Steve. "Besides, you can get it at sale price. Goes well with those new jeans. Lookin' good, kid. Now, stop falling in love with your image, Narcissus. Get a move on. I'm starving. Lunch is my shout."

Oh, yes, a birthday to be remembered. Now I was a well-dressed, ash-blond 18-year-old dude that I think some people looked at when I walked down the street. So far, none of Arvin's customers seemed to notice the difference, but meat workers, chicken killers, and timber millers can't be expected to notice everything.

CHAPTER TEN

Everton has not been so excited since the millennium fire-works display stuffed up, went into reverse, and set fire to the town hall.

Snout Hogg, Bazza Brown, and Freddie Gotz, another butt-ugly creep, have been charged with the murder of Spike Messenger. Lump Manning has been granted immunity from prosecution because, even though he was there, he took no part in the actual killing. Well, maybe he didn't, but I bet he thoroughly enjoyed the whole thing.

The cops picked the weakest link and worked on Lump. I hope I am not turning into a violent person, but a big part of me enjoys the thought of Lump slumped in a chair under harsh, hot bright lights. Three or four cops stand around and over him, threatening, using good old-fashioned strong-arm tactics, including being burnt in tender places with the odd lighted cigarette. Screaming his head off, he cries his eyes out...and then spills the beans! Working over a lump like Lump could be a whole heap of fun! Anyway, after a spot of torment and torture, Lump agreed to be the main witness for the prosecution.

Satisfaction guaranteed.

The strange thing is, I am now probably the only guy in town honest enough to say he didn't even like Spike. Spike is now the next best thing to a saint. A victim, a martyr to prejudice, a kid who was brave enough to be different. It makes me sick. Crowds

of those who had done their best to make Spike's life a misery—
and who were not much better than Snout, Lump, and the
rest—turned up at our courthouse to yell abuse and even throw
things at the three killers as they were led in and out of court to
face the charges. Killers? Alleged killers, really. Mind you, I am
not going to start working on their rights. I just wish we had
capital punishment. An eye for an eye and a tooth for a tooth.
Some bits of the Old Testament quite appeal to me. I'd hang the
bastards myself and enjoy doing it...well, if they're found guilty,
and they will be. Of course, the three of them have pled not
guilty and, so I am told, have said it was all Lump's idea. As if!
Doubt that Lump ever had an idea of his own.

My new best friend, Adrian Vanderlaar, has faced up to his
responsibilities in a way that I can only admire. We may not
have much in common, but I like him. He is rude, crude, and
naturally violent, but he is one guy, I have discovered, who has
got real guts and real courage.

Adrian certainly fully agrees with me on capital punishment
for Snout and the others, although he would, being Adrian, take
the process a few interesting and satisfying stages further.
"Yeah, hanging's OK. But I'd disembowel them first, like what
they did in the good old days. Yep, hangin' is sweet. Thought of
tryin' it out once. Would have been way cool."

I immediately thought of his three sisters. "Who were you
going to hang?" I showed a sensitive interest.

"Not 'who,' dumbo. Debbie, my big sister, had this pet rat.
Ugly bugger. But I changed my mind. Gave him to the cat
instead."

"That's horrible."

"No, it wasn't. It was cool. Well, it would have been, except
that rat scared the shit out of the cat." Adrian grinned. "It was

OK. Debbie never found out. She found him out in the garden and stuffed him back in his cage. Pity, really. It was years ago anyway. I was just a nice little innocent kid."

"Yeah, right! Very nice and innocent."

"But don't you reckon shooting might be more fun for Snout? You know, seen it in the movies...tied up to a stake and then let fire."

"It's too quick," I said, happily matching his bloodlust.

"Not my way, mate."

I should have known. "How?"

"Do the ankles first. Ouch! Then kneecap them, and then in the guts. Let 'em hang on for a while just to think of their, you know, sins. Then, whammo! Sweet, man. I'm a bloody good shot." He thought for a moment. "Least, I was."

"You still could be."

"Yeah, well, I'll be givin' it a go. Gotta give things a go."

Adrian was with me Sunday afternoon down at Arvin's. Business was slack. He said he'd come down for a pack of smokes, but I think he had come because he was lonely. He turned up most times when I was at work, flying down the hill in his chair, wind blowing through his hair. He had even mastered the art of doing a sort of wheelchair wheelie, a doughnut on the forecourt, well and truly startling any other customers. None of this took guts, but the return trip up the hill took every ounce of his courage. I could tell how much it must hurt.

It's not a steep hill, just a slow rise all the way—about a mile to the corner where he'd turn off. But it's a very steep hill if you are in a wheelchair, have only half a body to use, and that useable half still in the process of mending. I watched him the first time he tried it, imagining the pain as he zigzagged up 20, no more than 30 yards at a time. "D'you need a hand, a push..." I yelled out at him after he had agonizingly pulled himself up about 100 yards. "There's no one here."

He looked back at me over his shoulder and called back, "Piss off!" A snarl, really. He went at a snail's pace, sometimes resting, back bent and head hanging down, for two, three, four minutes. I doubt he shed a tear feeling sorry for himself. Maybe he cried from the pain, but certainly not from self-pity.

As far as I was concerned, this was one guy who could harbor wicked thoughts about rats anytime he wanted. On second thought, maybe not psychopathic ones.

In a matter of a few weeks he could master that climb in one go. Slow, for sure, but in one go.

This Sunday he had come for more than cigarettes or a pleasant chat on how to rid the world of Snout Hogg. "I go to court to get my sentence on Tuesday. Will you come with me?"

I looked at him and said, kind of slowly, "Yeah. If that is what you want. Why me? What about your father and mother?"

"They'll be there. It's just, well, I want someone else with me there. I can't say it easy, and I probably get it wrong. I want someone I can trust."

"You mean, a friend?" I wasn't going to let him off the hook too easily.

"I'm scared." He looked up at me. "Yeah. OK. A friend. I'm really shit-scared."

I could understand that. After all, he had taken the life of another person..."caused the death of another person" might be better.

"I've packed my bag," he said. "Reckon I'll be put away."

I didn't know enough about this stuff to say anything. Maybe he would go to jail, maybe he wouldn't. "If you want me to come, I'll come. Yep. I'll be there for you. What have you packed in your bag?" A natural curiosity. "Thought they gave you everything in jail."

"Just my toothbrush, pyjamas, stuff like that. Oh, and a couple of piss bags. Don't think they supply them." I must have looked puzzled. "Piss bags! You don't think I can go to the fuckin' toilet by myself, do you?"

"I hadn't thought," I said.

"There was this dude in the hospital, Christ knows what he had. Something terminal, I hope! He got on my nerves so bad that one day I picked up my full bag, chucked it at the bastard." He laughed. "Pissed all over him. Least then he smelt like a man!"

It is said that leopards are unable to change their spots. Adrian Vanderlaar was no exception to the rule.

One day as we watched from the garage as Adrian dragged himself up his hill, Steve said, "That kid's got a real future."

"As what?" An executioner?

"Look at him. That's some feat he accomplishes there. Upper body of his is getting well and truly developed. Arms, of course."

"So?"

"You told me he was king of the sport jocks at your school. Right?"

"He certainly was. Gifted. In about every code you could think of. Could run like the wind, jump, throw...enough to make you sick. He smoked like a chimney and drank like a fish and, from what he said, spent each and every night in the bed of a different girl."

"You can discount most of the latter."

"I don't think so. No one could make up some of the details he's told me. So what future are you talking about?"

"He is already a wheelchair athlete of some ability. Natural ability. You must have heard of the Paralympics? Seen them on the box?"

"Yeah. I see what you mean."

"I wouldn't mind offering to give him a hand," said Steve. "Must have a talk to him next time he bowls down here."

The strangest thing happened to me. It was as if I had taken a punch right in my gut. I walked off from Steve, back inside the gas station, not quite being able to work out what it was I was feeling.

When Adrian faced the judge, I was glad I wasn't the one facing this dude. I had a feeling this old guy could and would come up with more draconian punishments than Adrian and I had ever devised. I could only hope this was the judge that Snout and his mates would get to face.

"The accused will rise," said the bailiff.

"The accused may remain seated," said the judge.

"I will so rise, Your Honour," said Adrian, and he pulled himself from his wheelchair, his hands gripping the edge of the heavy table behind which he sat. The effort was enormous.

"Sit down," said His Honour.

"No," said Adrian.

His father moved to one side of him, and his mother, about the same size as my own mother, started to move to his other side. I sort of edged her out of the way, and his father and I helped him to stand up, supported him, his useless legs just dangling down. His lawyer stood on the other side of me.

"Have you anything to say before I pass sentence?" asked the judge.

"Yes, I have, Your Honour. Is it OK if I read it?" said Adrian.

"I don't know how I can stop you," said the judge, suddenly seeming a little more human. "What have you got to say for yourself?"

"Your Honour, I am sorry all through me for what I have done," Adrian read from notes he had made. "You look at me now and you see a man who can only ever have half a life. But at least I have got that much. Miss Lauren Brooks has got no life at all, and it is my fault. I can't say sorry to her, because she is not here. But I can say, I am sorry to her family. And I mean it from the bottom part of my heart. I don't want to be put away somewhere, but I quite understand if you have to send me to jail. That's all. I wrote these words myself."

"I can vouch for that," his lawyer whispered to Mrs. Vanderlaar.

"Sit down, young man. That's an order, and if you don't obey, I will hold you in contempt of court. That can also land you in jail. Sit." An almost-bellow from the judge.

Adrian sat. He was breathing hard and sweating from the exertion.

"I have given this case much thought and careful considera-tion," the judge said. "You have pled guilty to one of the most serious crimes on the statute books—a crime for which society, quite rightly and increasingly, calls for tough sentencing. That you have pled guilty, young man, is to your credit. You demon-strate that you are prepared to honestly and openly face up to your very serious behavior. Your guilty plea has also meant that the family of the deceased has not had to face a lengthy and painful ordeal..." We sat through a long spiel on youth drinking, youth driving, disregard for the safety of others and of self. All of it reprehensible, and with each one item alone enough to war-rant a sentence just short of disembowelment.

"I have read the lengthy and painstakingly prepared reports required by the court," the judge continued. "Your own injuries have been horrific, but with some courage, fortitude, and deter-mination you are, to all intent, making every effort towards phys-ical rehabilitation. The lower portion of your spine has been damaged beyond repair, and your limitations, physically, will be with you for the rest of your life." The judge looked Adrian directly in the eyes. "I note, young man, that there is already some concern locally at the speeds at which you appear able to propel your wheelchair. Take heed of my words." With that, he turned to address Mr. and Mrs. Brooks and members of their family, who were sitting in another part of the court. "The Court extends its sympathy to you both and to your family, and notes your generous comments in not wishing to exact vengeance on the young man who caused the death of your child...

"A custodial sentence, while not mandatory, is fully justified in this case. Adrian Vanderlaar, I hereby sentence you to a term of imprisonment of two years..."

There was an indrawn breath audible from Adrian and a gasp from his mother.

"However, in light of what I accept as true contrition and in light of the penalty you will continue to pay for the rest of your life, that sentence is suspended for two years on the under-standing that you will live where ordered—in other words, your home— and that your behavior during that time will be beyond reproach. Mr. Vanderlaar, you are free to leave the court. That is all."

Adrian broke down. It took both his parents and his lawyer a long time to comfort him and get him into a fit enough state to leave the court. Mr. and Mrs. Brooks came over, greeted Adrian's parents, and said just one or two quiet words to Adrian himself. Then we left the court.

Adrian and I had not been the only ones in court from Everton High. A dozen or more of our classmates had also packed into the place. They were waiting for him outside. They had ignored him for weeks. Now they were all over him. Pariah to hero in no time flat. Once again I edged away. He would have no need for me from now on.

"Well done, fella. Knew you'd swing it," said one of the guys. "Even in a wheelchair. Where's the party, man?"

Adrian looked at them all, a wicked grin on his face. "You know what?" he enquired of the whole group.

"What?"

"You can all fuck off," said Adrian. "Piss off, the lot of you. Come on, Carter, let's get rolling. Mum and Dad are waiting, and you'n me really do have a few drinks lined up. Dad promised."

How sweet! How very sweet!

Chapter Eleven

Not that the stream of my life right now had been very broad, but of necessity, it had to narrow even further for a short while. For a month, slightly longer, I shut myself off and away, and put my head down and studied. I now had no intention of further study, not after this year, not for a while. Like Steve, when he had left school, it was my full ambition to bum around for a year, two years, maybe longer. However, common sense told me that, eventually, further study would soon call, after that year or so, and the better I did now, the better it would be for me somewhere down the track when the time came to get back into harness.

I studied.

I sat the exams and knew I had done better, much better than just average, in everything. I was pleased with myself and knew in my heart that the results when they came would be as good as I hoped. I am not bigheaded about it. That's simply the way it was. After the exams I got ready to leave high school.

I had not seen my mother since the day before my birthday. I had a feeling that, if she could, she would come and see me. I didn't want to make her life harder than it was by going to see her. Since my father had bashed me up and kicked me out, I had not seen him. Not once. Nowhere. Give him his due—he had said I was no longer his son. And he had proved it. Hannah and Daniel? I probably saw them most days at school, but there had been no contact. I had never been close to my younger brother. He was a chip off the old block that was my father. I was happy to leave it that way. I prayed Daniel wouldn't harm or hurt too many others along his way. Who knows if I would be deeply troubled later on if we lost all contact. Somehow, I doubted it. Had never seemed to worry Steve that he had no contact with his family. It didn't worry me either. Blood thicker than water? No way.

It was in my last days at school that I began to wonder. Just a little. I sensed that I was being followed, and I was proved right. It was my sister, Hannah, who had been my stalker.

"Can I talk to you?" she asked. She looked nervously over her shoulder.

"It's 'May I talk to you,' and yes, you may. And don't look like a bunny waiting for the bullet. The old man isn't tracking you, and neither is his spy. Come in here. No one'll spot you." I took her into a small storeroom at the back of the main science lab. "What do you want?"

She looked little and scared, and I was reminded of our mother. "All I want to say is that it doesn't matter what, you will always be my brother, and please don't you forget that. There is nothing I can do about it now, but I don't want you to forget me."

What the hell is it about the women in my family and the ability they have to make me want to howl my stupid eyes out. I pulled myself together before the old waterworks spouted out a load. "You had better be careful," I said. "You are going against everything your father has taught you. You transgress not only his rules but those that you know, full well, are in the Holy Bible. Watch out, and hey baby, don't you worry. I know you are my sister, and I promise you this: I will always be your brother, even if I am an evil one. OK? And now you better go. You know what they say—walls have ears!"

Hannah gave a small smile. "Now I feel much better. I have tried to see you by yourself for a long time. It is not easy, with your friends all around you."

Friends? Hadn't thought I had many. "Well, now you've seen me. You had better not tell even Mother that you have. Now, off you go." I stopped. "Hey, come here," and I gave her a little hug, and she reached up and kissed my cheek.

"God bless you and keep you, Paul." Then she smiled at me. "You look super cool these days." She slipped out and, super cool that I was, I wandered off to whatever it was I should have been doing.

Things were to get more confusing before they became absolutely turbulent...

I went to see Principal Sparks to do the right thing, to say thank you, to get my leaving certificate from him, and to tell him not to expect me at the senior prize-giving evening.

I made the right noises, got my certificate—he could hardly withhold it—and he threw a spanner in the works. "I can't accept your excuses, Paul. You may be experiencing difficulties with your family but, regardless of that sadness, I expect you at the function."

"I don't have to go," I said bluntly, clutching my certificate.

"No, you don't. And I suppose it is beyond me to force you to turn up. I think you owe it to the school." He coughed slightly. "In most respects it has served you well, and you have served this place well. It seems you leave me no recourse other than to tell you."

"Tell me what?"

"You are our top scholar. Magnificent results, and all credit to you. I tell you this in strictest confidence and in an effort to make you change your mind: It is going to be a strange situation if you fail to turn up to accept your due rewards. I know your parents will be here for Daniel and Hannah. Do you not think it may be a good thing for them to see you in this particular light? Shall we just leave it at that for now? In other words, I expect you to do the right thing. By the way, it has not gone unnoticed how much help and encouragement you've given Adrian Vanderlaar. Good for you."

Top scholar! Whew!

"Bloody great, man," said Steve. "Crack open a bottle. Let's drink to it. May even find a couple of cigars somewhere. Time you tried a man's smoke. And don't hand me that shit about not going and all that crap about your ex–old man. Of course you're going. I'm coming with you. You can't deprive me of that. Good on you!"

"I don't think I could face him, Steve."

"The boot should be on the other foot, man. Far as I'm concerned, you come face-to-face with him, you can take your pick—knock him flat, spit in his eye, or just walk on by. My advice? Take the third option." He looked at me very hard. "It just may help your mother a little to see you there. Have you thought of that?"

I saw him, all right. Smug, self-satisfied, unctuous bastard. Man of God? Ha! He had no option other than to see me as I trotted up and down to and from that stage to accept a truck-load of goodies. And there were more than enough people on my side to make sure I got a good round of applause each time. I knew I looked good. And I looked happy. I stared the bastard straight in the eye every time I passed him. I even found the time and space afterwards when he was out of sight to give my mother a quick and furtive hug. Her face as she looked at me said it all. Yes, I was glad that I had gone.

No more school. I couldn't have been more pleased!

I started work full-time for Arvin and ran the whole place for 10 days so that he, Lalita, and the dreadful kids could have their first good holiday for years. They went back to Fiji, where they had all come from.

It was then that things started to happen.

I heard him yelling at the top of his voice long before he wheeled into the gas station, up the forecourt, and into the shop part. I was serving a customer. "It's happened it's happened it's happened it's happened." Adrian spun to an erratic halt, knocking over a display stand of chocolate. "Thank Christ, it's come back." He ignored the startled shopper. "I've had a hard-on! A hard-on!"

I thanked Christ I had an understanding customer! She put a hand to her mouth, giggled, accepted her change, and said to Adrian, "Good on you, kid." Laughing out loud, she left to spread the happy news. Takes more than a hard-on to shock most of Arvin's customers.

"Oops," said Adrian. "Didn't realize you weren't here by yourself. Oh, shit, man, you got no idea." He was trembling. "I had given up bloody hope, even though I worked on it like hell. But it's back! It's back! Shit, reckon I'd rather have that than the use of my bloody legs."

"Settle down and get to work picking up all that chocolate. No, I'm not going to help you." I wanted to ask just how he had worked on it but didn't want to run the risk of another customer arriving in the middle of what I knew would be a graphic description.

He looked at me. "You don't understand, and I thought you would." His lip trembled. "Can you imagine what it's been like for a guy like me—well, for any guy..."

Getting to know Steve, and Adrian, has sure worked to break

down a few inhibitions in me. "Of course I understand. It's brilliant! Guess you now got to work out where you're gonna put it. Eh?" Something I would never have said six months ago!

"Look, mate, no probs for now, at least.' He held out his hand. "Good ol' Mrs. Palmer and her five daughters can wring the old goose's neck—for now, anyway. You've no idea how good it feels." He looked at me. "Guess you're right, though. That won't last. Gotta find somewhere half decent to stick it. How d'you reckon I can get a blow job?"

"I don't know. You're the one told me they used to queue up just for the honor of giving you one. Must be one or two who would still help out."

"Nope. None of them cows. No way. They turned against me, all of 'em. Got to find me someone new. Wonder what a guy's like blowing another guy. Can't be all that much different if you close your eyes..."

"Be a bit more, well, bristly, I reckon."

"That's OK. Be surprised, there's quite a few bristly chicks around, not that I've...don't suppose you...nah. Course not."

"Don't bother thinking down that path." I turned away, thinking back, smiling just a little.

"How about old Derek from school?"

"I have no idea." I pointed to the phone. "Give him a call. You might be surprised."

"Hmmm, least he's got a helluva long neck and throat. And, well, I've got a big one."

"Goes without saying," I said.

"Could be OK. I'll give it some thought. Still," and he spun round in his chair. "Might be a bit premature. I've only had just the one."

"One what?"

"Hard-on." He felt between his legs. "Nuthin' there at the

78

moment. Still, reckon it'll be cool. Life in the old guy yet." He patted himself and grinned. "Did Steve tell you the other good news?"

"What? Has he had a hard-on too?"

"Funny guy. Ask me, he's the kinda dude that has a permanent one. Takes one to know one, they say."

"Well, maybe you better give him some thought if Derek turns you down," I said.

"Steve? You gotta be joking. Old Steve has gotta be the straightest guy around. You can always tell. Mind you, he'd sure be handy to do a quick one for me. Didn't he tell you I'm gonna be working for him? Full-time in his workshop. Some sort of apprenticeship training in how to turn old stuff into new stuff. Cool, eh?"

Cool? It was if someone had taken a knife, plunged it into my heart, and turned it till I had no life left.

The bastard! Why the need to be so secretive about it? Given the time I had spent with bloody Adrian bloody Vanderlaar, surely I would have been the one he should have talked over such major plans with. Working together? Oh, yes, very cozy. Swearing together? Yeah, I reckon! Nonstop foul language. Smoking together? Indeed! Laughing together...oh, to hell with it. If that's what Steve wanted, Steve could bloody have it.

Round and round inside of me, eating at my gut, consuming me, and all the time showing I didn't give a damn. Why, for chrissake, Adrian Vanderlaar? Why couldn't he have asked me if he needed someone to work for him? As least he wouldn't have had to trip over a damn wheelchair every which way he wanted to move. Why not me? Would have been nice to have been asked. A change from Arvin and pumping gas might have been very nice for me indeed. What was it about Adrian Vanderlaar that made him preferable to me—his housemate, his friend?

So, Vanderlaar's had a hard-on. Well, big fuckin' deal! What the hell would it have mattered if he had never had another one? Probably had more in the last three or four years of his life than most guys get in a whole lifetime.

Oh, yes, very cozy. The two of them together at work. The two of them together at play...well, at training. Christ, Steve had even bought an expensive stopwatch so he could time Adrian's runs. Runs? That was a laugh. All Vanderlaar could do, would ever do, was roll! Oh, yes, serve him right. I knew how to put a spanner in the spokes of even that wheel! I would do my very best, all sweetness and light that I am, to encourage Adrian Vanderlaar to drink more and smoke more than he had ever done...and stuff him with chocolate. Paralympics? Ha! All that sod would be good for would be the fat-and-flabby-and-coughing Olympics!

Oh, yes indeed, very cozy. Just a matter of time probably, and I'd be chucked out of Steve's out on my neck, and guess who'd be sleeping in my room! On the day that happened, I'd get the last laugh on Steve Peterson, big-time doer-upper of crap furniture. Oh, yes. He'd be sorry when I finished with his books on the computer. The bastard would end up owing more tax than Bill Gates has to pay, and with the click of a few keys, I'd show he had defrauded the tax guys of so much money that he'd end up in jail for 10 years. Quite likely end up in the cell they'd been reserving for his good buddy Vanderlaar, who, truth to tell, should be using it himself if we had a justice system that wasn't so soft on criminal cripples.

They wanted each other? They deserved each other! I deserved better!

But, being the person that I am, I allowed none of this to show. I didn't even say anything to either of them. I said it all to myself deep down inside me.

Chapter Twelve

"I've got to go up to the city for a couple of days," Steve said. "Business. Back Thursday night around 6, no later. You be OK here?"

"Yeah, sure. What do you have to do up there?"

"Oh, this and that," said Steve.

Secretive even about this. "Not a problem. Anything you want done?"

"Nothing to do, man. Plenty of food in the place. Practice your cooking." He grinned. "You need to."

"I do not." I smiled back at him. "I'm a perfectly good cook."

"Tell that to the birds...well, at least to any who have survived the last stuff you threw out on the lawn." He laughed at me.

Maybe Adrian Vanderlaar would prove to be a top chef. "My cooking doesn't kill as many birds as your damn cat."

"All right, all right, don't get sensitive about it." He held up a hand. "I've got to be fair. There was something you cooked last week that was actually quite edible. Can't remember what it was."

"Probably some toast," I had to laugh too. What on earth was it about this devil that made me turn to jelly inside every time he grinned his wicked grin, smiled his sweet smile, or laughed his loud laugh?

I could have gone up to the city with him if I had bothered

to ask. Arvin got back, paid me a small fortune for my managerial skills, and ordered me to take two days off. To be strictly honest, Steve had not known this would happen and that I would end up with time on my hands. Mind you, to be even more strictly honest, Steve had probably wanted to take Vanderlaar with him anyway.

I'd show the brute!

I mowed the lawns. I mowed them perfectly with a nice crisscross pattern that took hours to achieve. I carted away a mountain of accumulated garden rubbish. I trimmed all the edges and raked the gravel driveway—again, into a nice pattern. Steve loved his garden, and after I had finished with it, even I could see why. It is beautiful, as gardens go. I cleaned all the windows in the house, both sides of them. All this took the whole of one day.

The next day I got up good and early and started on the dog. Audrey wasn't too happy at first, but she entered into the spirit of things. The ugliest dog God had ever created, Audrey had been rescued by Steve when she was a little puppy and in the process of being savagely beaten by some dude who should never have been allowed to own a dog. Steve is good with lame dogs! I shampooed, scrubbed, bathed, and brushed Audrey until even she thought she looked good. Wasn't much I could do for Mr. Cat, even if he had let me. He saw what was happening to poor old Audrey and sprinted for the hills.

After everything outside passed muster, I drove to town and bought a cooked chicken, a bag of salad and other deli stuff, and a nice slab of cake. Then, just to show I was now old enough, I bought a bottle of good wine. This is the sort of cooking I am quite good at.

I drove home, parked the car, re-raked the drive, gave Audrey another brush, and even fed Mr. Cat, who sat at a sensible distance, eyeing me suspiciously. For a moment I toyed with the idea of giving him a nice bath. I didn't.

Then I set to work on the inside of the house. Even though I say it myself, I am ferociously good with a vacuum cleaner, and with that and a feather duster, I soon had the inside of the house as spic and span as it had ever been. Even polished up the bathroom and got rid of all of Audrey's hair from around the bath and down the plug hole. Then I started to put away things that should have been put away...jackets, coats, sweaters, and in the two bedrooms, bedding that was no longer needed now that the nights were warm. Yes, indeed, I'd show the brute just what a house-and-garden treasure I could be. Like, how the hell would Adrian Vanderlaar ever manage to bathe Audrey—much less mow lawns. What a laugh. To be fair, though, knowing Adrian, he'd probably find a way to do both. It can be a bit of a problem being fair.

Steve's bedroom did not need much tidying. A few sweaters into the wardrobe and a pair of socks into the laundry basket. He had taken a couple of blankets off his bed, folded them, and they sat neatly on the floor in a corner of his room. I couldn't see where I might stow them, except in a chest that he had at the bottom of his bed used more as a table, and with a littering of books, magazines, and odds and ends that I had already tidied and dusted. I took all this junk off and put it on the bed, and opened the chest and looked inside.

Then I knelt down and started to look more closely and then, God forgive me, I couldn't help myself. I started to go through the stuff that Steve had stored in his chest. It took me a long time. Finally I got to my feet, shook my head, and rubbed my eyes. I put everything back inside his chest as near as I could remember it had been, and then, I don't quite know why, I put the two blankets in on the top, closed the lid, and replaced the books and all the little bits and pieces.

I went outside in the sun, sat on the bank of lawn that ran down from the house, pushed Audrey away, and hissed at Mr. Cat. I smoked one and then another cigarette, even though I had given up smoking for good. I just sat there in the afternoon sun, thinking for some time, putting together pieces of the jigsaw of Steven Peterson's life that I had discovered in his chest. Secrets? It seemed he had a few things to be secretive about.

Later I went back inside and set the table ready for dinner, had another cigarette, and waited for Steve to come home.

"My God, man, you've worked miracles! How the hell have you found the time? I feel guilty just for having driven up that driveway...and look at those lawns!"

My heart near burst. The bastard. "Didn't take too long," I lied.

"Jesus! Look at her!" He crouched down to greet Audrey, who slobbered all over him and probably tried to tell him what a mean bugger I had been to her. "Looks like he's even been nice to you," he said to Mr. Cat, who had no intention of being ignored by his owner.

"Put it this way, I didn't give him a bath." I grinned. "Arvin made me take a couple of days off. Thought I may as well put them to good use. I've cooked us dinner."

"Oh," said Steve. "That's nice. I had thought we might go out for a bite. Still, if you've been slaving over a hot stove all day, I may as well take the punishment." He smiled, and we walked inside to the living room. "Hell's bells, look at that."

I had picked a few somethings from the garden and plonked them in a vase on the coffee table. "Well, you like a few flowers," I said.

"We'll be able to like them for a bit longer if you put a bit of water in with them too."

Mean bastard! "Ouch!" I said. "Thought I'd remembered everything."

"Wow!" said Steve, when he spotted everything on the table. "You've sure been cooking. Well, almost cooking." He looked at me and smiled. "Hey, my man, thank you."

"It's nothing," I said. Yeah, right. Nothing?

We sat down and munched until it had all gone and there was nothing left to throw to the birds except the chicken bones. The bottle of wine had served to chill us both out a little, and to me, it seemed almost like old times. Just him and me. And then the worst possible thing happened. Steve pushed a small gift-wrapped package to me across the table. He leaned back, grinning, then lit a cigarette and said, "Well, open the bugger."

I opened it. "Shit!" I said with elegant simplicity, and drew the watch out of its box. "This must have—"

"Yes, it did," said Steve. "You need a decent one. Call it, oh, I dunno, a pre-Christmas present, a little something for being top-dog student. Just call it something I wanted to get you."

Confusion. Utter bloody confusion! Gold and silver, all of it gold and silver. The watch breathed money. I put it on. It fitted my wrist perfectly. It looked truly wonderful against my browning skin. "I don't know what to say."

"You like it?"

"Of course I like it."

"Then just say thank you."

"Thank you. No one has ever given me anything like this before." In all truth, I doubt that I had ever known anyone who could have afforded to give me something like this. I took it off and examined it again, turned it over to see what was on the back. Might have been better if I hadn't. It had been inscribed PAUL. A GREAT FUCKIN' FRIEND. STEVE.

"Took a bit of fast talking to get the guy to do the inscription. But he finally came to the party."

I looked at him and I smiled shyly and said, "There is

nothing more that I can say other than 'Thank you.' "

He grinned again and he winked at me. It was at that moment that I fully realized and owned up inside myself as to how I felt about him. It was nothing to do with him giving me an expensive gift. Nothing like that. It was just him being him. I stood there not knowing what to do or what to say. So what if the bastard had secrets? Maybe he had his reasons, maybe not. Only he knew. So what if he preferred the company of a disabled dude in a wheelchair over mine? That was his right. That was his choice.

Besides, above everything else, the way I thought about him was, most certainly and beyond any doubt, not going to be the way he thought about me. This was a man. A real man. A man's man. No wonder he had plumped for Adrian instead of me. The two of them, well, they just knew they were men sort of instinctively. I could never show—never, ever, ever show—how I truly felt about him. The feelings I had for him could not be the feelings he had for me and would have to be hidden, kept to myself, forever and ever. I was no more than a waif and stray he had given a home. I was as Audrey had once been; probably Mr. Cat too. Probably a whole long parade of the down-and-out and needy he had met up with along the way. Sure, he liked me. He liked his dog too!

Steve opened another bottle of wine and set about polishing it off while I tidied the dinner stuff away. When, finished, I sat down opposite him, he said, "I'm whacked, man. Shouldn't have opened this bottle. I'm gonna hit the sack."

He stood and looked down at me. "Glad you like the watch." He acted as if he wanted to say something more but just gave a little shrug and took off to his bedroom.

A minute or so later he came back out. "It's turned a bit cold tonight. What have you done with my extra blanket?"

I hesitated but only for a split second. "Um...put 'em in that chest at the bottom of your bed."

He looked at me. He looked back into his bedroom and then back at me. He knew from the look in my eyes that I had seen it all. A hand came up to his face and then through his hair. It started as a sort of agonized groan and rose in crescendo to something approaching a scream. "You, you...you, you...you, fuckin' little bastard...you been...you been into my shit...you been through my stuff, you fuckin' little snoop..." His rage grew and he came towards me. "Had to snoop and spy into stuff that was none of your fuckin' business, you dirty little creeping Jesus..."

I was standing. "I...I didn't..." but he gave me no chance. I had only ever seen one other person as angry as this! I started to tremble and to shake. I also started to look for an escape route. No chance whatsoever of escape. He was backing me neatly, inexorably into a corner. I backed away until I could back no further. All the while his string of obscenities and vitriolic invective rained down onto me, into me, smothered me in its ghastly intensity. My mouth opened and closed, opened and closed...but nothing would come out. Nothing at all.

"Took you into my fuckin' home, and this is what you do. You make me sick, you fuckin' little goody-two-shoes Jesus creep, mealymouth me on the one hand and stick it to me with the other." Then finally he was on me and he pushed me hard, very hard in the shoulder. I knew that more would come and that, this time, I had to defend.

I pushed him back. I pushed him back just as hard as he had pushed me. That shut him up but only for a moment. "Hit me, would you, little sod. I got news for you. You. I eat little boys like you for breakfast..." He pushed me again, even harder.

I had seen this guy at work and knew that I didn't have one

earthly chance of holding him at bay, much less besting him. This time, however, I was not going to go down without a fight. This wasn't my father. This was...only God knew what! I pushed him back; he balled a fist and hit me. I did the same to him. At first it was almost in slow motion. He was beside himself with rage, and I was beside myself with fear. We did tit for tat for probably half a minute. He looked me in the eye, and I stared straight back at him. Our faces were only inches apart. Steve Peterson's anger was such that he was barely recognizable. His deep-blue eyes were black as night and very hard.

I don't know what spilt the whole works over the edge, but spill it did and then we were at it, the two of us, hammer and tongs and no holds barred. Punching, shoving, yelling, well roaring, panting and gasping, gouging at each other, and both of us trying to hang on to our balance. We were evenly matched in size and probably in strength, but the advantage was with Steve. He knew the right moves, the nasty moves in ways that I had never dreamed of. He hurt me, and I did what I could to hurt him back. I knew that eventually his cunning would alter the balance and I'd be gone, history. That I stayed on my feet for as long as I did amazes me. But in the end he caught me off balance, and I fell and he sprang down onto me, pummeling the shit out of me until all I could do was my slight best to protect myself.

I got in a few good blows, and I think I nearly screwed off one of his ears. But finally the advantage was his, and he held me, pinned to the ground. I gave up then and I knew, just looking up at him and at the strangest look in his eyes, that he too was almost spent. Swiftly, neatly, he swapped the hand that held one of my arms for his knee. And then, very lightly, almost gently, he brushed the hair from my forehead with his free hand and whispered, "Right, you little bastard. I have wanted to do this from the moment I set eyes on you, and I'll do it once before you boot me in the balls and fuck off." He bent down onto me, mouth open, and kissed my lips, forcing my mouth open and his tongue right in and down.

It was as if my whole body had been hit by a bolt of lightning. My back arched; I'm sure I forgot all about breathing. I didn't close my eyes, and with every molecule of my exhausted body I responded as fully as I could. This wasn't easy with both my arms still trapped. Finally, Steve tried to pull away. I tore my arms half out of their sockets in my refusal to let my mouth break from his. He drew away, staring at me as if transfixed. Then, releasing all bits of me that he still held trapped, he rolled over onto his back.

I rolled to face him, and then, using one of my wounded arms, I came up above him, smoothed his forehead, and said, "I am not going anywhere and I am not going to boot you in the balls and I am now going to do what I have wanted to do so very much that it hurts worse than what you just done to me." I came down onto him and kissed him and kissed him and kissed him. Then I held him in my arms and comforted him, the bastard bully, while he howled his eyes out! Then we kissed again.

Now, it's early days—very early days for me and kissing—and I feel sure I have much to learn. But no kisses will ever live in my memory in the way that those first three kisses surely will: the sweat of our bodies, the acid taste, the hunger and the heat in both of us.

That Steve and I had physically hurt each other was apparent. We were exhausted, absolutely spent, and we didn't say much as we cleaned each other up, patched each other up, and even straightened up upended furniture. I made us tea, and we sat sipping it side by side on the sofa. We didn't talk. Scarcely a word. Finally he said, "OK, man. Come on. Bed." A tight little smile. "My room. I've got the double bed. And then we sleep, nothing else. That what you want?"

Well, I most certainly wanted a heap of other things, but I did know that on this night they were quite out of the question. He undressed me. He stripped me. "Hmm," he said, looking down and with another little smile. "Good size," and, blow me down, for all my exhaustion the good size got better! He undressed himself, we got into bed, and for the whole of what was left of that night, I know we just held each other. I know, because we were still holding each other when morning came. I might have felt sore all over, but I had never felt better or happier in my life.

The morning matched how I felt. It was glorious. Early sun shone in through the uncurtained window, and everything gave promise of a great day to come. I snuggled down even closer and more securely into Steve, breathed deeply, and went on feeling perfect contentment.

"Ouch!" said Steve, rolling over. "Got me there, you little devil."

"You're awake?"

He turned towards me, smiled lazily, and said, "Been awake for hours."

"You're a liar," I said.

"You can't prove it," said Steve, and ever so softly he took my face in both his hands, turned it to fully face him, and kissed me very, very gently on the mouth.

If he wanted electricity this early, he'd sure get it! I moved to get a degree more vigorous.

"No no no," said Steve. "Just lie back." Very softly. "Just relax." I felt his fingers start to travel down...oh, God!...oh, dear God! "There." Then he said, "Hell's bells, have you got a jack-in-a-box down there? Quicker than a bloody on-off light switch! Got a life all its own."

My cock had waited a long time for this. Not surprising it had a life of its own! I just lay back and groaned as his fingers, gently at first, slow-motion slow, got to work on me. Then his face, oh, those bristles, kissing me all the way down and under the covers until his mouth got there, and I could feel his tongue and I did not know what to do other than to hang onto him like grim death and dig my claws into his back...and then I came...and I went on coming...

"Well, my man," Steve said as he came back up to face me, a wide grin on his face. "That gun of yours shoots quite a load!"

After that, I let my fingers do the talking, travelling them down his fit torso and into what seemed to be an endless forest. I would be a fool to say that instinct guided me, rather than the example he had just set. Or maybe it was a combination of the two. Whatever, the result was very much the same.

"Oh, yes. A little bit of practice, my man, and you'll make one highly desirable lover. Not too bad at all for what I suspect was a very first time. Oh, fuck, I shouldn't say shit like that! Thanks, man. That was truly great."

I took his hand and slid it back down the length of my belly. "Cool, eh?"

"God in heaven! Not already! Oh, well, I guess being 18 does have one or two advantages."

We slept again for another hour or so, until I was ready for another go. However, it wasn't to be. "Nope," Steve said. "You and me have got some serious talking to do."

"Can't we do it in bed? Give me one of your cigarettes. I need something in my mouth." I winked at him.

Steve lit two smokes and handed one to me. "I mean serious talking," he said. "It will be far better if we are showered, dressed, and sitting up at opposite sides of the table, facing each other and having a cup of coffee..."

"I don't think it would be better than this. It couldn't be." I felt so relaxed, so drowsy, so safe...even if I had been more than a bit bruised over much of my body by this guy who now made me feel this way. "OK," I finally conceded. "Have it your way. Can we come back to bed after we've had the serious talk?"

"I've heard of quick character changes but reckon this one beats all records. Get up! That's an order."

Chapter Thirteen

We sat at a table out on the verandah in the morning sun—showered, dressed, respectable, facing each over coffee and bacon and eggs. I was surprised that it was only 8 o'clock.

"Right, then," Steve began. "We've had a bad night and a good night, a bad time and a good time. A few things need talking through. A bit hard to know where to begin."

"I am deeply sorry if you think I spied on you. I didn't. All I was doing was looking for a good place to put away your blankets. I didn't even think—"

He held up a hand. "It's OK, Paul. Well, it is and it isn't. I should have had the guts to burn all that shit years ago. Didn't have the guts back then and haven't had 'em since. Don't know how much you did see, but here's the bare bones of it at least." He looked at me.

"You don't have to tell me anything. It doesn't matter."

"Yes, it does. I didn't bum around when I left school. I went straight from school into the navy. Officer cadet. Did very well. Commissioned as an officer. Started the climb. Quite likely would have gone on doing very well if I had climbed over a few more bodies on the way. Who knows?" He gave me a cold grin. "Probably have ended up a fuckin' admiral. Oh, yes, I had all the right stuff."

"You sure looked good. Those photos! Hell, you looked great."

"See! You are a kid, aren't you? There is a million miles between looking good and being good. Yes, I did look good. As arrogant a little shit as the armed forces ever spat out—and they sure spit out a few. Did you see all the stuff in there?" He nodded in the direction of his room.

"Saw the uniforms all folded and looked at the framed photos. There was other stuff I didn't touch."

"So you saw him then?"

"Him? Who do you mean? There's a heap of you in your uniforms or on ships with other officers and guys."

"I meant the more social ones."

"One or two with you partying and everyone with arms draped round each other and looking as pissed as frogs."

"Newts. Pissed as newts."

"Whatever. Pissed."

"Had you looked more closely, certainly if you had spotted the more personal photos, you would have seen my arm round one of the guys in more than just a friendly fashion. I'll cut a long and quite boring story short. I fell for a guy. More than that. I fell in love with him. He wasn't an officer. He was an enlisted man, younger than me by two, maybe three years." Steve got to his feet and started to pace up and down the deck.

"You don't have to tell me," I said.

He looked at me. "Yes, I do. You are the one person I must tell, and not just because of what happened last night. I should have told you this a long time ago."

"I don't understand," I was puzzled.

"Shut up and listen. You soon will. This was, well, a few years ago. Yeah, sure there were gays in the military. Always had been and always will be. It's easier today but not all that much. It was OK, even back then, unless you got caught. We got caught, right in the middle of the fuckin' act and by quite the wrong person...but that's another story. If you got caught at sea—and we were on a frigate and we were certainly out at sea—the book got thrown. I got out and away. Don't ask me how I managed it. No one at all knew it had been me screwing the other poor guy. They certainly knew what he had been up to, poor little bastard. The sweetest kid. All of 19 years old. Well, they screwed him every which way and they bullied him, threatened him, and for all I know, tried to beat out of him the name of the guy he had been with. I found out later they even tried to bribe him. I have a feeling there were likely a few suspicions in the minds of one or two older dudes, officers, who either hated my guts or wanted to get into my pants."

"I know what you are going to say."

"Yes. No matter how hard they tried, he did not let on it was me. He got fired. Oh, not for having it off with another guy...they couldn't do that. They trumped up something else. The navy is good at doing things like that. The kid was defenseless. No one to speak up for him. Now do you see where I am heading?" Steve sat down opposite me again and rested his head on his hands. He smiled slightly.

"Yes and no," I said.

"I could have saved that kid, that young guy, my lover. I could have saved him. If not fully, at least in part. All I had to do was stand up and say that I was the other party. But I didn't, did I? Oh, no. I saved my own precious hide and let someone else be sacrificed. I did not stand up to be counted when I should have. I didn't have the guts. I let someone else take it in the guts for something I had instigated, started. I quit the navy as soon as I could, but even then, I got out honorably, didn't I? Not him. He wasn't so lucky."

"I don't think—" He didn't let me get any further.

"Don't start on with any crap about understanding or not

knowing or whatever. I couldn't take that from you. You are sitting here in front of me today as a fuckin' living rebuke to me! You stood up on behalf of someone else. You let yourself be counted. You took a shitload of fuckin' crap right on the chin without ever thinking of saving your own hide." He smiled wryly. "You're a man, kid. I was that proverbial bloody mouse. Oh, sure, I looked good in the fancy dress. Just a pity the cool costume was covering something hollow. End of speech. Say nothing. I'll have a bonfire someday soon and burn the lot, everything in that damn box. Everything."

"Just one thing? Well, two things."

"Go on."

"First, you can't go on bashing yourself up over something that happened a long time ago when you were still young. And second, what happened to the other guy, your friend?"

"I don't know, Paul. In all truth, I do not know. For a long time I didn't look. When you're into saving your own hide, nothing much else, no one else really matters. A long time later I did try to find him. At least find out about him and if he was all right. It was as if he had disappeared off the face of the earth. Not all stories have happy endings. Well, now you know...and that's only half of what we have to talk about. Get inside and make me some more coffee, you sex-crazed little stud. Still feel the same about me now I've told you all that shit?"

"Of course I do." I smiled at him.

"Stupid fool," he said. "Don't you have to go to work?"

"Not until 4. I'm doing the late stint. What about you?"

"I'm the boss, kid, and don't you forget it. No. Stuff work today. Need to spend it with you. Need to repair a bit of the damage you did to me, you savage little bugger," he rubbed an arm. "I'll go in for a few hours when you go down."

"Cool," I said. "I'll make us that coffee. You want more eggs and bacon?"

"Good Lord, no! Look, you want to fry up more, fire ahead. I'll just sit here and smoke. Better for my health."

I couldn't for the life of me see why we had to do all this talking. Would have been far better to have just gone to bed for the day. There are obviously certain penalties to be paid falling for an older dude. Well, this one, anyway. Maybe I could see why he went on whipping himself over the young sailor, but whatever he said, it did not make Steven Peterson seem less of a man in my eyes. Sure, it had been sad, but hey, we all make mistakes. No part of me wanted to hear any more about this slice of Steve's life. We were here, now, here today. He, we, should be looking forward. But I hadn't quite counted on the next bit.

"Why can't we just take things as they come? You want me. I want you. Period. It's simple."

"When did you realize you were gay? When did you know?" he asked.

"At least you haven't asked me if I'm sure I'm gay and just working through a time of confusion blah blah blah and still searching out my sexual identity blah blah..."

"I wouldn't insult you." He laughed. "Thank God I didn't try!"

"Two, almost three years ago."

"You sound certain."

"I am. I found that guys attracted me in a way that girls didn't. I couldn't keep my eyes off them. No matter how hard I tried I couldn't stop getting, well, excited. You've got to realize, Steve, that this was bloody awful for someone like me, coming from my sort of family. Here I was, just a kid, attracted to something—a way of life, I guess—that I had been brought up to regard as evil, an instrument of the devil." I sighed. "I can't talk about it lightly. There's a heap of torment in feeling that you are utter filth..."

"No loving God ever intended it to be like that, Paul." He spoke softly. "You poor kid. You must have been so bloody desperate. So alone. You of all people, Paul, are not utter filth."

"I think I am coming to see that. There are still struggles." I lightened. "But hey, I give in easy, don't I?"

"Not all that easily. Has there been anyone else? Not that I have to know."

"I don't care what you want to know. No, there hasn't. Yes, telling the truth, there was a guy who really did get me going and who did me the great favor of me finding out what I was. Guess who? Who d'you think it was?"

"How the fuck would I know? Snout Hogg?"

"Got it in one."

"Not the poor Messenger kid?"

"God, no. I admired old Spike, but I couldn't stand the sight of him. Spike had no trouble at all spotting what I was, telling me, pointing it out to me and goading me on to be honest and do something about it. I never did because there was no point."

"Did Adrian ever know?"

I looked at him. "You bastard," I said as I took one of his cigarettes and lit it. "Of course he didn't know. I'm not a fool. Hiding my feelings caused me a bit of pain...a lot of pain. I think those feelings were going, had gone, even before he had his accident," I smiled widely at him. "The situation was hopeless anyway. I think he must have told me about every girl he screwed. Believe you me, it really was quite some score. Any feelings I had for him were dead dead dead when I met you. So there. Now you know."

"I knew. You realize that Adrian worships the air you breathe."

"So the bastard should. I've stood by him for a while now. You know he's had his first hard-on since his accident?"

"The whole town knows. Been back in town less than a day and even I know. He's not one to keep anything private."

"He's been looking for someone, doesn't matter who, who'll give him a blow job. Your name came up but then got discarded."

"I'm devastated," said Steve. "What's wrong with me?"

"Oh, according to Adrian, you're the straightest guy in town. But you like Adrian, don't you? You're giving him a job, coaching him..."

"So-o-o," A long, drawn-out breath. "That's what's been eating you. The green-eyed monster, eh?" He laughed and he laughed and he laughed.

"No," I said.

"Oh, yes," he said, and went on laughing. "Good old jealousy. You've no idea just how happy it makes me feel to find out you have at least one weak spot, Mr. Less-Than-Perfect." He chortled away. "Look, there's only one guy around here who may, and I stress, may, be for me. It's not Adrian. Of course, I'm a sucker for a pretty face, and he's sure got one of them. You saw those photos of me in the chest. Not an ugly dude in sight. Yes, I'm shallow. Yes, of course I like Adrian. He's got guts, spunk, call it what you will. Courage. He's been a bad bugger, will probably go on being a bad bugger in some form or other...but he's not sitting back in that wheelchair and feeling sorry for himself. He's owned up to the dreadful harm he has caused and shown himself willing to take the consequences right on the chin. These days he's up and at it and doing his level best to do something about his life. I know in my bones he'll work his guts out for me. I know in my bones that one day he'll beat the bejesus out of any other guy in a wheelchair. But I am very glad to hear he ruled me out of contention for a blow job. It's not *his* dick I want to feel near me in bed."

I don't know why, but I felt ashamed. In fact, I felt very ashamed. All I said was "Adrian's a good guy."

"That's stretching it a bit. Forget him for now. There's just one other matter that we do have to talk about..."

This time I was the boss. "And I know what it is. I know what you are going to say. I don't need to hear it, and it doesn't matter. You can take the 13 years that separates our ages and shove it where the sun don't shine. Right?"

Steve did the old goldfish mouth. "Er—"

I played his role. "I've said it." I held up a hand. "I'm just a kid and you're an old man. Well, old man, you can stop talking to me like you were my damn father. OK?"

"If—"

Now I was laughing. "Oh, yes, I fully realize that when you are 93 I'll be 80. That's incredibly sad. Like what self-respecting 80-year-old wants to be seen with someone over 90."

"Point taken. Don't worry, man, I'm the first one to admit I'm not over the hill. Give you a run for your money anytime, even at my advanced age." Steve smiled at me. "Now, fella, we got a few things need doing."

"Yeah, I know." Very broad grin. "Back inside, eh? Come on."

"Not quite what I meant," said Steve. "You're insatiable."

"Oh." I must have looked a bit crestfallen.

"To hell with it," said Steve. "Come on, you little stud bull. Guess we can explore each other's tender spots for an hour or so."

"That all?"

"Come on." His arm around my shoulder, we walked back inside and went to bed. It's amazing, truly amazing, just how well two guys, feeling as we felt, can explore each other's tender spots with such care. We were both too tired to get into amazing gymnastics. After about an hour of tender exploration—and one or two slightly less tender moments—we fell asleep. It was late morning before we finally surfaced, and I got ready to go at it again.

"Oh, no you don't. Not this time. Time enough up both our sleeves..." Steve began.

"Yeah. Our whole lifetimes."

"Don't say things like that," he looked at me. "Oh, shit, don't look at me like that. Just...well, don't tempt fate. Just, well, let's go with the flow and take each day as it comes. Jesus, I'm the first guy you've ever tumbled into bed with...there are others out there, kid."

"Not for me," I said.

"I'm delighted to hear it," said my lover. Lover!

"I'm a one-man guy, Steve." He just looked at me with an amused smile on his face, then lit a cigarette. "You can give me one too."

"I thought you had given up?"

"I have. And I'll give up again tomorrow."

"Heard that one before. Bloody idiot, even starting. Look, you've got to go to work in a few hours. Get your backside out of bed and get that front room cleaned up. You made all the mess."

"Did not. You made your share. You knocked over those lovely flowers I picked just for you. I remember." I tried to sound indignant.

"Rot. Besides, I've got to kill a sheep. Christmas coming, and we need a bit of the next best thing to lamb."

"You going to kill a sheep? Can I come too?"

"You bloodthirsty little bastard." He looked at me and another broad grin spread across his face, and he slipped his hand down under the sheet. "You little devil. Violence turns you on."

"No," I swallowed. "Course it doesn't. Um..."

"I thought so," said Steve, very slowly. "Right back then. I was right..."

"About what?"

"Me dealing to Snout the swine in the best way possible. I knew I was right. That turned you on, didn't it?" He smiled. "God, you've no idea how close I was, back then, just how close I was to jumping you, Mr. Goody-Goody Christian. Hell, maybe I should have."

I got out of bed and stood, stark naked and quite limp, and looked down on him. "Violence as such, Steve, does not turn me on..." I saw and felt in my mind a picture of the violence that had led me to being here. Connections. I felt sick.

I think Steve read the look on my face. "Just joking, Paul," he smiled. "Come here."

I flopped down across him as he lay sprawled on the bed. "Ouch!" we both said together. Then I said, "Well, all right, I'll be honest. It's just that, well, seeing you, only you, doing certain things sort of, well, sort of gets me going. That's all."

"A very mild case of bloodlust, I think. Come on," he pushed me off. "Let's go and kill a sheep. I guess it makes a kind of biblical-style sacrifice, if nothing else."

"OK," I said.

Steve keeps a few sheep in what he calls his orchard. Uses them as lawn mowers. The fruit trees are all still babies and have protectors around them to stop the sheep munching on them instead of on the grass. The beasts live very satisfactory and happy lives for as long as they are allowed to lead them. They are kept for meat as well as for their lawn-mowing abilities.

I am not sentimental about animals. Certainly not about sheep. I'm a very happy sheep eater. We walked up the railing fence separating the garden from the orchard. The sheep, unsuspecting fools all of them, ambled their way towards us.

Steve often fed them odds and ends of leftovers and, quite often, the results of my cooking. They weren't getting any today. "OK, man. Your choice. Which of the ladies is it to be?"

"That one." I pointed out the fattest. It seemed to be the fairest way to go.

"Old Gertie? Oh, not old Gertie. I'm rather fond of old Gertie."

I knew he was having me on. "Too bad. You gave me the choice."

"Come on, Gert," Steve said. "The young brute's signed your death warrant. Time to go to greener pastures."

Now, if violence really is a turn-on for me, the slaughter of Gertie the sheep was a very minor one. "Wow, that was quick," I said, part of me admiring his skill. Part of me saw Gertie as an animal designed for this purpose. Sheep? You eat them, you wear them. But another part of me saw my mother, my sister, my brother, myself—and my father! "I don't think she felt anything." I gulped.

"Of course she didn't." Steve looked up at me and winked. "No need for Gert to suffer as long as Snout Hogg. She was an innocent."

"I suppose you're going to tell me next your grandmother taught you how to do this too."

"She most certainly did." Steve started to haul dead Gertie towards a small shed. "Wide range of interests old Granny had. She also taught me how to do petit point embroidery, how to knit, and, oh...how to play the saxophone."

It only took a few minutes to remove Gertie's sheepskin coat. Slightly longer, I must admit, to remove her insides. I didn't enjoy this last bit and decided to give up eating meat, having sex, and bloodlust forever...well, for a while.

Chapter Fourteen

Life was different. At home, just Steve and me—it was wonderful. I had never been this happy, had never felt this happy and fulfilled in my whole life. It wasn't that we spent the whole of our time snuggled down in bed. Sure, we spent more than a few hours there, quite a few more than a few hours. And it was wonderful. But just as wonderful as exploring each other's bodies, and everything that goes with the sex life that two athletic and adventurous guys can enjoy, was the time that we spent getting to know each other. Quiet times out in the sun in the garden, doing things together, or sitting beside each other out on the deck in the dead of night and trying to figure out the starred sky.

Life was no different. We still had to get out of that great double bed in the mornings and get off to work, toil away all day, and then come home and get stuck into cleaning up the mess that the two of us were quite good at making. The ordinary stuff of anyone's life.

Yet I wanted my life—the lives of the two of us as a couple, our living together, and how we felt about each other—to be screamed out loud so that everyone would know. I wanted the whole world to know we were a couple, indivisible, an entity. I didn't want our love and how I felt about it to be hidden away. I had something to crow about, and I wanted to crow. I wanted to yell out to the whole damn world, "Steven Peterson and Paul

Carter are a queer couple and bloody proud to love each other, and if you don't like it, world, then you can bugger off!"

That this didn't happen was not of my choosing.

"What you are saying is you are ashamed of us," I said to Steve. "Why the hell do we have to stay in the bloody cupboard?"

"Closet."

"Closet, cupboard, who gives a stuff? There's a bit in the Bible—"

"I'm sure there is," said Steve.

"You don't light a candle and put it under a bushel. That means you don't hide something good."

"I think it means more: You don't light a candle and put it under anything if you don't want to start a bloody great fire!" Steve smiled. "Look, man, you took absolute shit just for standing up for a gay kid. You come out in the open around here, around Everton, and you not only announce you're queer but you're living happily with another one—a much older one too— it'd be a bucketful of shit for you and a ton of it for me. Believe me, it's far, far better to stay in the damn cupboard."

"Closet," I said.

"Don't get smart with me," he said. Then he stopped smiling. "I have no reason to think that your mother has anything other than a hard life. Do you want to make it harder? You would, you know. Put two and two together. Don't just think of yourself. Now, come here."

"No," I said, but I moved towards him.

"Stop being a spoilt little boy." He put his arms around me. "Come on, let me feel the bits and pieces of you I love feeling and that you like me feeling."

"Feel away," I said, sighing. "It's not fair. Oh, God, it's not fair."

"You're right. It isn't fair. Look at you. A kid who simply wants to yell out to the whole fuckin' world that he's in love...oh, shit, if you must do it, well, then do it."

I broke away from his hug and stood back from him just slightly and looked into those eyes that could swallow me just about whole. I wanted to cry, but I didn't. "I love you. I know I love you, Steve. I know I'll never, as long as I live, love anyone else like this..."

"Never say things like that," said Steve.

"Bugger you, I'll say them if I want to. I mean it. I mean what I say. And you love me. Don't you?"

"Nah. Just pretending," he said.

"Well, you're pretty good at pretending. Yeah. You love me."

"If you say so." Steve smiled back at me.

I got serious. "All right. What you think is best is not quite what I want, but I will go along with it. I'll go along with it for now. But let me tell you now, I will feel as I do in six months time, a year from now, 10 years, even—"

"Shoot! As long as that?"

"Don't treat me like a kid, Steven. I'm just letting you know that I am not going to go on forever hiding away...hiding what it is I know I feel for you. I want to share my feelings with the bloody world, even if the bloody world doesn't want to know about it. OK, so Everton isn't ready? Is that what you're saying? Well, it's damn well going to be one day. It's just got to be."

"Sit down," said Steve. "Right here by me. Come on." He put an arm round my shoulder. "Let's be happy in the here and now, just as we are. We've got a whole heap of learning to do, both of us, about what it's like to live, fully live, with another person. We've got to learn about what makes us tick. Mind you, I reckon we're getting there on that score."

"But—"

"Shut up, man. This is a long speech. We've got the time, this coming year, to do just that. No great stresses and no great strains. What happens after that? I don't know, and you don't know, either—"

"I do so know." I caught the look in his eyes and shut up again.

"You're going to have further study. That study is going to take you away from here for some long time. If things work out for us, for you and me...well, maybe it will take me away too. I'm not shackled to this place, even though I love it." Steve looked around the small house. "What I am saying is that maybe we go away together. Wherever you head, wherever we may end up together, is going to be light-years ahead of this strange little community in its way of thinking. If you still feel the same way then, well, my man, then will be the time to stand up and yell to whoever gives a shit whatever it is you want to yell. Get my drift?"

"Yes." I looked at him. "Go on. You said this was a long speech."

"Just remind me to get physical with you when I've finished," Steve said with a laugh.

"Yes, please. I can't wait."

"By 'physical,' I meant something like strangulation."

"Cool. That magazine I found under your bed the other day said that slow strangulation was a great way to bring on orgasm."

"The last thing you need to discover is any kinky way to orgasm. One look at your dick and it spurts!"

"You can talk! Anyway, finish off what you wanted to say."

"That's about it, Paul. Just don't ever think I want to hide away or that I feel ashamed of what I am or feel that anything that you and I have going is anything other than wonderful, pure, clean—maybe not always clean—but exactly the way it should be. And don't worry, there are dozens of places not too far from here where we can be seen together and be accepted for who and what we are. Can't wait to drag you into a few of them, if for no other reason than to see the looks on the faces of the other dudes not as lucky."

"That's not very Christian, Steven."

"And stop calling me Steven," said Steven.

"What sort of places, Steven? And when can we go, Steven?"

"Ready for your last orgasm, are you? I'm certainly ready for the strangling," he said as he looked out of the window. "Hell's bloody bells, and now it's raining. I was going to force you to mow the lawns. What I say is, why keep a cock and crow yourself!"

I grinned very broadly at him and nodded towards the bedroom. "Let's go and find out why. Bugger the lawns."

Chapter Fifteen

Christmas. No going to work for 10 whole days. All the factories around the gas station closed down, and Arvin did the same. Steve followed Arvin's great example. It was just so very sweet. A stretch of time just for ourselves in which to do nothing at all except lounge around in the sun, eat, drink, and enjoy our own company. Just the two of us.

"You want to go to church?" asked Steve, two or three days out from the big day. Mid-morning and we were still in bed. "Like, you go if you feel you want to."

"Why? You want to come with me? Feel like a new experience?"

"Like hell," said Steve.

"Look, it's like this, Steven: I have been to church enough times in the past 18 years to last me a lifetime. God does not expect me to go to church ever again. Even if he did, I am not going. I do not want to go to church. I am not going to church. OK?"

"Fine by me." Steve laughed at me. "We'll have a fully pagan festival. Got to get us a tree, too much food, and an ocean of booze."

"Yep. That's my sort of Christmas from now on. Jesus wasn't even born at Christmas anyway."

"I'll take your word for it. Better let the pope know—give the old guy a break."

"The pope, Steve, is the next best thing to the Antichrist.

We did learn that at the New Life. We are not in touch with the pope."

"Given your feelings about New Life, it may be time for you to bond with him."

"I haven't got time. Besides, you've told me I've got to help you kill those poor old hens for Christmas dinner. That's sure pagan! A very happy Christmas they're going to have. Not! What have they done to deserve it?"

"Stopped laying eggs, that's what, useless old dames. They knew what to expect when I got them. They are sure going to taste good. Talk about fat. Now, get out of bed and make the coffee. It's your turn."

"OK, OK." I rolled out of the bed, pretended to struggle to my feet and, stark naked, staggered out of the bedroom and looked straight into the face of Adrian Vanderlaar as he was about to hammer away at the glass front door. "Jesus!" I yelped, and ducked for cover back into the bedroom.

"Jesus? Well, he's made his Advent a few days early," Steve mumbled, rolling over. "What have you done this time?"

"It's... it's...it's Adrian out there, and he's seen me."

"Then get back out there and let him in," ordered Steve as I pulled on a pair of shorts. "How the hell did he get here? Didn't hear a car. Settle down. He hasn't seen anything."

"The bugger's seen me. Like, well, he's had an eyeful of all of me."

I could make nothing out of what Adrian may have seen or not seen from the look on his face as I let him in. Adrian Vanderlaar had half killed himself just getting out here. He had wheeled his whole way out from town, unaided, up the hills, over the gravel of our road, up the winding drive. Somehow, only God knew how he could have done it, he hauled himself and his chair up the steps and onto the verandah. He was exhausted, and it showed. "I done it. I got out here all by myself" was all he muttered for quite a while.

Steve tended to him while I made coffee. "Your parents know you're here?" he asked Adrian.

"Nope," said Adrian, still gasping, grabbing for breath.

"Stupid little bastard," said Steve. "Just rest for a while. I'll phone them." He did, talking for quite a while.

"I had to do it," Adrian said to me when he was about half recovered.

I was going to say that, no, he didn't have to do it at all and that either Steve or me—or his parents, for that matter—would have brought him out here. Then I looked at his strained and dusty, dirt-smeared, and sweating face. "Yeah. Reckon you did, Adrian. Good on you." It wasn't beads of sweat rolling down his cheeks, it was tears. But I pretended not to notice.

"If I've got to live all my life like this, I've got to do things for myself. If I can't, then, shit, I gotta croak myself. Simple as that."

Steve was off the phone. "You've got to learn to take one step at a time, you silly, dumb prick. Asking for a bit of help does not signify you're useless. Your mother and your father were frantic with worry. A note saying you'd taken off for a wheelchair marathon at 5 in the morning was hardly designed to set their minds at rest!"

"I got your Christmas shit, pressies for you," Adrian said, brightening by the moment. He's not an easy guy to keep depressed.

"I don't care if you've got the baby Jesus Himself," said Steve.

"Couldn't find the bugger," Adrian said with half a grin.

"Cut the crap, Adrian," said Steve. "Paul, cart that old wood-en seat into the shower. It should fit. Wheel him in. If he's dragged himself this far, he can drag himself out of his chariot and into the shower. I know he doesn't want his parents running around after him, so I'll duck into town and pick up his painkillers, muscle relaxants, and the other stuff his mother reckons he needs."

"You don't—" began Adrian.

"Shut up, Adrian," said Steve. "You got yourself out here under your own steam to our place. Now you're here, you'll do what you're told. Then he turned to me. "If he doesn't behave, Paul, you have my full permission to use whatever strong-arm tactics you choose."

"Cool," I said, flexing a few muscles. "Go on, Vanderlaar, start doing what you're told not to do. I'm lookin' forward to the strong-arm bit."

"Give him another coffee first and pour me one too," said Steve. "I'd better fling on some clothes. When he's had his shower, and if I'm not back, put him in er...your room, Paul. You'd better have a rest, wheelchair guy."

Adrian looked as if he wanted to argue. Sensibly, he didn't.

"I'm buggered." Adrian had wangled himself back into his chair, and I had steered him to the bathroom. He looked up at me. "Don't know if I can do it." He hung his head. "Whew!" And then he looked up at me again and said through gritted teeth. "But reckon I will. Piss off, Carter. I'll call out if I need help."

"Promise?"

"Piss off."

I don't know how he did it, but he did. It took him awhile and he didn't call out for help. I could hear him, could hear the shower, could hear the occasional low groan or muffled yelp. Finally, he wheeled himself back into the sitting room, clean, much brighter-eyed, and dressed in the old towelling robe that I had worn a long time ago after my first shower in this house. "OK?"

"Sure."

"I need a smoke," said Adrian. "In my pack." He nodded towards his sort of wheelchair backpack.

"Hell, Adrian! You got bits of a rifle in here. What the…"

"Was going to make the most of my trip and shoot the Christmas Bunny up where you and Steve reckoned there were heaps of them."

"No such thing as the Christmas Bunny."

"Sure there is. It's the bugger that got missed at Easter. Light me a smoke."

I did as he asked, and then, over his loud and foul protests, manhandled his wheelchair and him with it into what had once been my room. "You can get yourself onto the bed. Look, just have a rest for 10 minutes. Give me a chance to tidy up the bathroom and have a shower. Then I'll be back and I'll bring you a beer."

"You bloody better," said Adrian. I turned to leave the room. "Hey," he called out behind me.

"What now?"

"It's cool by me, you know."

I turned back, looked at him, and knew that he knew. I felt myself go hot and then cold. "What do you mean?"

"You and Steve." He had a mile-wide grin from ear to ear. "Think I'm fuckin' thick, both of you. Been written all over you for weeks." He looked around him. "Besides, anyone can see this is not your room, and I've only spotted one other with a bed in it. Takes a fucker to know a couple of fuckers." He was laughing. "Got one thing wrong, didn't I?"

"Got what wrong?" I started to smile.

"Could've asked old Steve for a blow job after all. Would have made his day. Could've knocked me down with a feather when I finally put two and two together. Look, dude, I don't give a shit, not anymore. More things to life than worrying about who or what someone wants to fuck. Ever tried a sheep?"

"No. Have you?"

"Yeah, Darlene Hewitt from school. Always thought she looked a bit like a sheep. Sort of woolly."

"You'd know."

"If you and Steve are happy the way you are, that's cool by me," said Adrian. "You're both my mates. You've proved that. Bloody good mates. Just don't expect me to join in for a threesome."

I pulled a face at him and winked. "Don't you mean a two-and-a-half-some?"

"Clever dick, ha ha. When you bring that beer back, you tell me what it's like takin' it up the bum. Want to know all about it."

"Bugger off."

"Well, you should know all about that." Adrian laughed out loud. "Reckon I will have me a little snooze. Just don't you sneak back when I'm having a zizz and take advantage of a nice, straight, innocent young guy like me. I know what you queers are like."

One tiny step out of the cupboard!

So much for a quiet pre-Christmas at home, just Steve and me! Adrian stayed for a day and a half, and would have stayed longer if we hadn't bundled him up and carted him back to his own home. "Best bloody Christmas I've ever had. Screwed the necks of five poor old hens and knocked off 23 bunnies." He sighed a satisfied sigh.

"Yeah. Very bloody Christmas," I replied. "I got to mow the lawns and dig up a bucket of new potatoes."

"You got a few rabbits."

"Yeah. Great! When you'd let me have a go. I think I got two." Not that I was worried. I seemed to have lost much taste for knocking off or harming other living creatures, even if rabbits are pests and we are going to eat Gertie and the old hens. Purer I may be, but I'm not ready to be a vegetarian.

"Why can't I stay?" Adrian asked Steve.

"Because we don't want you," said Steve.

"That's not very nice," said Adrian. "You two want to get stuck into it, eh?" he winked at Steve. "You can get down and dirty with me around. I want to watch."

"I'm sure you do," said Steve. "Horny little buck like you better be careful. Might just spot something you'd like to get stuck into yourself."

"Doubt it," said Adrian pleasantly. "I'm just interested in a...what's it called? Yeah, that's it...in an academic way. Studying sex is a deep interest of mine. Like, well, what do you do when you want to—"

"Mind your own bloody business," said Steve. "Roll over to the fridge and get some more beers for us, and try not to drop them this time. Make your miserable life useful. While we're on the subject of sex, how's it going with the hard-ons these days?"

"Mind your own bloody business," said Adrian. "I don't discuss my sex life with gays. Just makes 'em all sad about what they're missing." He gave us a big smile. "If you must know, the old boners are not going too bad at all. Poppin' up at all odd times."

"Good for you, man," said Steve.

CHAPTER SIXTEEN

Looking back, this was as merry as that Christmas would get.

We rid ourselves of poor old protesting Adrian and went home to do nothing at all other than sit in silence and watch the sun set above the trees at the end of the garden. We were just quiet, happy, and alone, the two of us. Then the phone rang. "Leave it," I said to Steve.

"Not on Christmas Eve, man," said Steve. "Besides, it could be Adrian's mother saying he's deliberately left something or other he desperately needs and he's wheeling his way out again. God help us." He went to answer the phone. "It's for you," he said, bringing it out to me.

"Adrian?"

"No. Take it."

It was Hannah, my sister. "I must be quick, Paul. Mum is in the hospital. She...she has had a heart attack..."

"What...what?" A sort of a bark.

"Mum has had a heart attack. Just a little one. She won't die. I don't think...she is at the hospital. Go...go...go and see her now. Got to go now to church...Daddy...church. Go and see her now. We won't be there now..." Then the phone went dead.

I called straight back to the house, my old home. Nothing. The phone gave out the engaged signal.

Steve was at my side. "What's wrong?"

I told him. "Must go. Got to go and see her now."

116

"Of course. Come on. I'll take you. She'll be OK. You'll see. Come on," Steve urged.

I dithered. "Dunno. Dunno, do I. She...he—"

"Come on. Change out of your shorts. Grab a sweater. It's cooling down, and you're shivering." Steve said, taking charge.

"Of course you can see her. All by herself at the moment. She's going to be fine. Just a little bit groggy and a bit knocked around," said the nurse.

"Knocked around?"

"Apparently she had a little turn, a minor warning sort of coronary. Fell and got a wee bit bruised here and there. Just a bit groggy, and of course, we've got her hooked up to this and that to monitor things."

"I'll wait outside," said Steve.

"Don't tire her out," said the nurse. "She's had a little bit of a fright, and we've given her a sedative."

Her eyes were closed. She appeared to be dozing. I just stood there looking down on her. She looked so small and worn-out, so plain and pathetic. I stood there with a fiery fury rising in me that seemed consumed the whole of my body. "Fell and got a wee bit bruised..." Like fucking hell she had fallen! With all my heart and soul, I knew where these bruises had come from.

My mother's eyes opened. She blinked a few times as she looked up at me, almost as if she couldn't believe what she was seeing. "Paul?"

"Hello, Mum." I bent down, gave her the tiniest of hugs with, really, just my two hands, and then I kissed her on her forehead. She winced.

"Had a bit of a nasty fall, love. Some funny sort of turn. Silly..."

I pulled a chair up to the side of her bed and took her hand

and just held it and stroked it. Then I spoke. I spoke very softly. "No, Mum. Not this time, Mum. Ssshhh…" She tried to speak. "Don't lie to me, Mum. I know what happened. He did this to you and now he's gone off to pray to God and give thanks for the birth of His Son. Oh, yes, he's bashed you up good and proper this time, but he won't be asking for forgiveness for that. Ssshhh…it'll be all right. You mark my words. Now, you take your time and you tell me what happened. If you don't tell me the truth, then I am going to go to the police right away and they can find out what went on…"

"Oh, Paul…it's not…oh, I am so tired."

"I'm sorry, Mum. I know you are tired, but this time you are going to tell me. If you don't tell me now, next time you might end up dead. Simple as that."

"God in His infinite wisdom…" and then she took my hand and started to stroke it. In her small voice, little more than a whisper, she told me. "It was just a small parcel I was packing, odds and ends I had saved up, put aside and hidden away…I wanted to…you…your father found me. I had offended him. He was so upset. He had every right…he did…"

Then Steve was beside me, and he had an arm around my shoulder comforting me, "Hey, man. It'll be all right. Your mum's going to be all right."

"You don't understand," I howled. "He caught her packing a parcel to bring to me. For Christmas, for chrissake. And that's what she gets for it. It's me, Steve. It's still me. He might pull the damn trigger, but I'll be the one who kills her."

I don't know how, but my mother found the strength to take a little bit of control. "We'll have no more of that silliness, son. Goodness me. Now wipe those eyes of yours. And in front of Mr. Peterson. Really!"

"OK, Mum." I looked hard into her eyes. "I know you love

him. Well, you say you do. I know you do everything he says for you to do. You obey him. He's not worth it, but that is your decision, your choice. But now you listen to me. I don't know how I am going to do it, but do it I will. I am serious about the police. I have to do it. They have to know. And I am going to come and see you and Hannah, whenever I want to, and he is going to let me." Brave words! How? "And if you want to come and see me, you come and see me. Understand?"

She was certainly well enough to look skeptical! "If you say so, son. And now I am a little tired. Besides, your father, Daniel, and Hannah will be back to see me after worship. I think I need a rest now."

"Come on, Paul. Your mother's right. She certainly needs a rest," Steve said, siding with her.

So did the nurse, who came in and told us that enough was enough and that it was time for her to check that Mum was still alive.

"Jesus!" announced Steve. "Talk about bad timing!" We walked out of the front door of the hospital, down the steps, and right into the path of my father, brother, and sister.

This time he did not take me unawares. I was ready. Well and truly ready. I pulled away from Steve's restraining hand on my arm and went to face my demon as he advanced towards me, face reddening and eyes glaring, bulging.

"How...how did you know..." my father said. "Been to survey the damage you've wrought? I hope you're happy. Benighted woman she may be, but she deserves better than you, you wicked and fornicating scum, slime of Hades and shame of my life!"

"The damage I've wrought?" and I yelled him down. Out of the corner of my eye I spotted Hannah fading into the shadows and my brother behind her. "What the hell do you mean, the damage I've wrought?" A bellow from me. "Come on! Come on! Get stuck into me, why don't you. What you always bloody do to all of us..."

His mouth opened and closed a couple of times. Suddenly, he became aware that there were a few other people, visitors probably, coming and going from the hospital. "Shut your mouth. Shut your filthy mouth," he hissed.

I was right up to him now in a blazing and dramatic fury. "No!" I screamed. "No, you bloody bully, I will not shut my mouth. Not this time. Go on! Go on! Get stuck in. Belt me up. Belt me up again!"

"For God's sake...keep your voice...keep your...there are people—"

"Right, Father. There are people. Scared of what other people may hear, what they may think, Mr. Holy Man...My Holy-Bloody-Hypocrite," I added. I lowered my voice just a little as I took him by the front of his jacket, pulling the fabric tight and forcing him back six, eight feet away and off the path so that I had him backed up against the trunk of an old tree.

"Paul! Come on, Paul. He's not worth it." Steve was pulling at me.

"Get out, Steve. This is my fuckin' fight." I shrugged him away and then forced my face right up so close to my father. I could see the veins throbbing in his temples, and his breath smelt sour. My teeth weren't just gritted, they were clenched. "You!" A sneer at him. "Yeah, I'll keep my voice down, but you'll bloody listen to what I'm going to say to you. You'll listen to every word I've got to say and you'll keep your fat gob shut. Man of God! Ha! You're not a bloody man of anything. You beat me up and kicked me out and I fuckin' took it from you and didn't lift a sodding finger..."

"Er...er...urg..."

"Shut up! Shut up or I'll strangle you with your bloody tie. That's my mother sick in bed in there, and you've bullied and bashed her, bullied and bashed me and the other two for as long as I can remember. You've bashed her up for the last bloody time, you bastard. That's why she's there now. And the other two know it." I raised my voice again. "And don't you worry, you chicken-liver chickenshit, I'm not going to do the same to you, even though every bit of me wants to hammer you so hard you wouldn't walk for the rest of your life." I raised my voice again, and he looked nervously from side to side. "Yeah! That's got you worried, hasn't it, Mr. Man of God? Don't want the bloody community to know you beat up your wife and kids, do you?"

I relaxed my hold just a little. He tried to pull away from my grasp, but I tightened it again. I had the upper hand and I was going to keep it. "You'll change your habit of a lifetime, or you mark my every word, every person in this town is going to know it. Every little bit of it!" I sneered at him. "You...you call me scum! You call me the slime or the bloody slug or whatever of Hades! God, you talk rubbish! It's you who's evil, you...you bloody beater of a poor woman whose little finger is worth more than 10 of you! Stick to bashing the Bible. That's all you're bloody good for! You keep your dirty hands off my mother."

"What do you want?" he croaked.

"What do I want? I'll tell you what I want and what I'm going to do. When I've done with you, I am going straight to the cops, and you know what I'm going to tell the—"

"No. No. They won't—"

"Believe me? Oh, yes they will. I'll bring them here, one way or another. They'll soon see that most of those bruises on her could never have come from a fall. A fall? I'll bet she fell, poor Mum. I'll bet you, you bastard, knocked her over. Put the boot in on her, did you? Did you?" I was now in some danger of strangling him. Good!

"She...she won't—" he managed in a sort of grunt.

"Lay charges? You reckon? She may not have to when they fully examine her. What you've done to her will speak for itself." I knew it was a bluff. "And even if they don't, Pastor Carter, I'll lay charges against you for the beatings, the abuse you've given Hannah, Daniel, and me. You mark my words, they'll be keeping an eye on you forever and ever amen. And, oh, yes, just think of the gossip. Even you know how the bad news rips through this place...like wildfire." I released him a little bit but not much. I looked over my shoulder and called out, "You, Daniel! Come over here!" I didn't think he'd do it, but he did!

"You better let Dad go," he muttered.

"Don't worry, I'll let him go. You don't think I want to keep him, do you? Come here where I can see you." I looked at my brother. He looked so scared. I couldn't hate him, even though part of me wanted to. "I'm holding you responsible too. I know you can't stop him." I shook my father just to make the point. "I know you can't stop him." I repeated.

"Well...what then?"

"If he shows the slightest sign of ever attacking Mum or Hannah, or you, ever again, you get on the phone, you get me, wherever I am. If I am not around, you call the cops. I don't give a stuff about honoring your bloody father. This one hasn't done anything to earn our honoring of him. Understand? Do you understand?"

"Yes," he spoke in a small voice.

"You had better understand. If I find out he's ever done anything to any of you ever again and you haven't told me—"

"I understand," said Daniel.

I let my father go and backed slowly away from him, feeling

Steve's hand on my arm, gently pulling me from the place.

My father straightened himself, his jacket, sort of tilted his chin, and began to intone, " 'For their worm shall not die, neither shall their fire be quenched; and they shall be an abhorring unto all flesh.' So is written the word of the Lord our God—"

Which pushed me to the edge. "So help me, God," I screamed as Steve's light touch became an iron grip and Daniel grabbed my other arm. "I'll smash his fucking face! I will!"

It took the two of them to get me away from the place, out to the car park, and into Steve's truck. By then my rage was barely under control.

"I will tell you, Paul. I promise." Daniel leaned into the passenger-side window. "Trust me."

I looked at him. There was nothing, nothing at all smug or smart about him as he stood there, worried, serious. "Good man," I said as Steve started the engine and Daniel moved away. "Hey, Daniel."

"Yeah, what?"

"You know where I am. Come and see me, and..."

"What?"

"Happy Christmas."

"You too, Paul." He turned to walk back to Hannah and his father.

"Let's go home," I said to Steve.

Halfway home, he stopped the truck on the side of the road. He took me in his arms and just held me. I needed that hug.

High in the hills on a mountain track on a still, still day. It has been clear, but now it's slightly chill and mist wisps through wind-stunted trees. We stop, Steve and me, and his arm is around my shoulder. We look down from the track into the depths of a small and densely brown pond of water. So still, seeming so deep. Bottomless? That's what they always say, and such is the fable of mountain ponds. I pick up a handful of stones from the grit of the track, and we watch, intent, silent and together, as one by one I throw them into the water and the still surface ripples and goes on rippling.

A pebble in a pool.